"And  A Great Secretary."

"What?" Sophie glared at him. "I'm the best secretary you've ever had, and you know it!"

"Who the devil railroaded me into attending that meeting at the barbecue place? Who was it who insisted that it was in the best interests of the company to get involved in community affairs?"

"All right, I admit I might just possibly have influenced you to some small degree, but—"

"Oh, come on now, don't be so modest," Fate taunted. And then he sighed and raked a hand through his hair. "Look, Sophie, this isn't solving our problem." Where was his old secretary, the quiet, efficient woman who'd anticipated his needs before he'd even been aware of them himself?

There was something about his relationship with Sophie that was different lately. He couldn't put his finger on it, but he'd been around enough artillery to recognize a potentially explosive situation when one confronted him.

Dear Reader:

Welcome! You hold in your hand a Silhouette Desire—your ticket to a whole new world of reading pleasure.

A Silhouette Desire is a sensuous, contemporary romance about passions, problems and the ultimate power of love. It is about today's woman—intelligent, successful, giving—but it is also the story of a romance between two people who are strong enough to follow their own individual paths, yet strong enough to compromise, as well.

These books are written by, for and about every woman that you are—wife, mother, sister, lover, daughter, career woman. A Silhouette Desire heroine must face the same challenges, achieve the same successes, in her story as do in your own life.

The Silhouette reader is not afraid to enjoy herself. She knows when to take things seriously and when to indulge in a fantasy world. With six books a month, Silhouette Desire strives to meet her many moods, but each book is always a compelling love story.

Make a commitment to romance—go wild with Silhouette Desire!

Best,

Isabel Swift
Senior Editor & Editorial Coordinator

DIXIE BROWNING
Fate Takes a Holiday

Silhouette Desire
Published by Silhouette Books New York
America's Publisher of Contemporary Romance

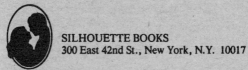

SILHOUETTE BOOKS
300 East 42nd St., New York, N.Y. 10017

Copyright © 1988 by Dixie Browning

All rights reserved, including the right to reproduce
this book or portions thereof in any form whatsoever.
For information address Silhouette Books,
300 East 42nd St., New York, N.Y. 10017

ISBN: 0-373-05403-3

First Silhouette Books printing February 1988

All the characters in this book are fictitious. Any
resemblance to actual persons, living or dead, is
purely coincidental.

SILHOUETTE, SILHOUETTE DESIRE and colophon
are registered trademarks of the publisher.

America's Publisher of Contemporary Romance

Printed in the U.S.A.

Books by Dixie Browning

Silhouette Romance

Unreasonable Summer #12
Tumbled Wall #38
Chance Tomorrow #53
Wren of Paradise #73
East of Today #93
Winter Blossom #113
Renegade Player #142
Island on the Hill #164
Logic of the Heart #172
Loving Rescue #191
A Secret Valentine #203
Practical Dreamer #221
Visible Heart #275
Journey to Quiet Waters #292
The Love Thing #305
First Things Last #323
Something for Herself #381
Reluctant Dreamer #460
A Matter of Timing #527

Silhouette Special Edition

Finders Keepers #50
Reach Out to Cherish #110
Just Deserts #181
Time and Tide #205
By Any Other Name #228
The Security Man #314
Belonging #414

Silhouette Desire

Shadow of Yesterday #68
Image of Love #91
The Hawk and the Honey #111
Late Rising Moon #121
Stormwatch #169
The Tender Barbarian #188
Matchmaker's Moon #212
A Bird in Hand #234
In the Palm of Her Hand #264
A Winter Woman #324
There Once Was a Lover #337
Fate Takes a Holiday #403

DIXIE BROWNING,

one of Silhouette's most prolific and popular authors, has written over thirty books since *Unreasonable Summer*, a Silhouette Romance, came out in 1980. She has also published books for the Desire and Special Edition lines. She is a Charter Member of the Romance Writers of America, and her Romance *Renegade Player* won the Golden Medallion in 1983. A charismatic lecturer, Dixie has toured extensively for Silhouette Books, participating in "How to Write a Romance" workshops all over the country.

Dixie's family has made its home along the North Carolina coast for many generations, and it is there that she finds a great deal of inspiration. Along with her writing awards, Dixie has been acclaimed as a watercolor painter and was the first president of the Watercolor Society of North Carolina. She is also currently president of Browning Artworks, Ltd., a gallery featuring fine regional crafts on Hatteras Island. Although Dixie enjoys her traveling, she is always happy to return to North Carolina, where she and her husband make their home.

One

"Buy you!" Sophie exclaimed, her eyes widening. "You mean you want *me* to go to the auction and bid on *you*?"

Fate noted with growing interest the telltale flush that appeared on her cheeks, the way her pink, neatly trimmed nails turned white with pressure as she gripped her pad. Unless he missed his guess, Sophie Pennybaker's poise, long a legend at KellyCo Dye and Finishing, had just been rather badly shaken. And he'd been the man to crack that all but impervious facade, he thought with a glow of satisfaction.

Meanwhile, back to business. It would never do to be caught gloating. "If—and I do mean *if*, Mrs. Pennybaker—if I agree to have anything at all to do with this auction of yours, you're going to have to agree to do your part."

"I'm afraid I couldn't afford you, Mr. Ridgeway," Sophie said faintly. "The bids usually go quite high, and..."

"I promise you, I'm no more eager to get involved than you are," Fate assured her. This unseemly hankering to get involved with his secretary was bad enough, without getting mixed up with local politics. Having moved south only a few months ago, he was still trying to get his bearings while he did the job he'd been sent to do, which was cutting out the deadwood and streamlining the whole operation. And dammit, it wasn't easy. Nothing in his experience, from M.I.T., to Air Force, to Harvard Business School, had prepared him for Turbyville, South Carolina, a town of some twenty thousand friendly souls who seemed in no particular hurry to saunter into the twentieth century.

Having fallen heir to this sexy paragon of a secretary didn't help much, either. His powers of concentration were shot. What Sophie Pennybaker didn't know about this business wasn't worth knowing, and she had a way of anticipating his needs that made his job a hell of a lot easier. At the same time a guy would have to be either dead or neutered not to find her distracting, and Fate was neither.

The phone on the desk between them rang, and he snatched it up and pushed several buttons, swearing under his breath all the while. Sophie's lips tightened. She'd have answered it for him if he'd given her half a chance. The man had no more patience than a flea!

While Fate talked to the New York office of the new owners, Sophie lowered her gaze to the few notes she'd taken before the subject of the Dunwoody auction had come up. They might as well have been Sanskrit. All she could see was that wicked grin of his.

Darn the man! She'd been doing perfectly all right with old Mr. Potter, never mind that he was half-senile, that he always reeked of cigar smoke, and that he had a tendency to chase the clerks and typists down the hallway when his gout wasn't giving him fits. Sophie had done most of his work for him while he'd called her his *girl* and bragged to all his cronies that he had the "best li'l ol' seckettary in the state of South C'lina."

At least he was harmless. And rather sweet, actually. There was nothing sweet about Fate Ridgeway, and as for harmless—!

Fate slammed down the phone and stared at her from across the desk. The gleam in his dark eyes might have been mistaken for personal interest by someone who didn't know him very well. Actually, he had asked her out to dinner once, shortly after he'd come to town. She'd declined, of course. Politely. Since then he hadn't bothered her.

Yes, he *had* bothered her, but that was her problem, not his. He'd made no further attempts to put their relationship on a more personal basis, and for that, at least, she was grateful. The last thing she wanted to do was to throw away sixteen years of seniority just because some here-today-gone-tomorrow executive made it impossible for her to do her job properly.

"If that's all, Mr. Ridgeway, then I'll get on with—"

"About the auction," Fate said, his voice overlapping hers as they both spoke at once. "If it's the money you're worried about, forget it. Naturally I'd expect to foot the bill."

"Mr. Ridgeway, it's not the money. It's—I just can't do it." Sophie felt herself stiffening up again, and she made a deliberate effort to relax the muscles in her shoulders. Those were the ones that were usually rock hard by the time she got home from work. "I'm not a very gregarious person, Mr. Ridgeway."

Actually, the thought of even attending such an affair, much less joining in the festivities, was utterly, absolutely, completely unthinkable. She wouldn't do it. Not even for the Dunwoody Home for Unwanted Children, more tactfully known for the past few decades as Dunwoody Farm. Just let her make a bid on a bachelor, and the town tongue-waggers would have a field day! *Is that the only way you can get a man, Sophie? Better make sure this one comes with a guarantee!*

Fate's chair squeaked as he tipped it back, and Sophie made a mental note to have it oiled. "Let's get something straight here, did you or did you not get me into this mess, Mrs. Pennybaker?" His tone of voice was not intended to make her feel more secure.

"The committee asked me if you were married when they were—um, revising their list. I told them I didn't believe you were."

"You knew damned well I wasn't," he corrected grittily. "I suppose you blame me for that revision?"

Sophie considered a spot on the wall to the left and slightly above Fate's head. It was safer than looking directly at him. "In all fairness, you can't be blamed for Mike Jessup's getting married last month," she replied. "But the list of bachelors KellyCo originally sent in to the Dunwoody Committee's planning board has shrunk considerably since they first contacted us last fall."

"My fault, of course," Fate put in smoothly. Meaning he'd fired two of the three other bachelors who'd been scheduled to go on the block, one for dishonesty and one for gross incompetence. The chair squeaked back into normal position. "Let's understand one another, Mrs. Pennybaker. If I agree to go along with this crazy scheme of yours—"

"It's hardly mine," Sophie protested. Piercing eyes, that's what they were. All her life she'd thought it was just another cliché, until that Monday morning three months ago when L. Lafayette Ridgeway had first looked at her across this very desk.

"You gave them my name."

"They already knew your name," she corrected gently. "I merely confirmed their guess that you were unmarried. At least as far as I knew."

"As far as you knew," Fate echoed, mockery in the crooked twist of his mouth. "Mind telling me how you arrived at that conclusion?"

Instinct, she retorted silently. No married man could possibly look quite that predatory. "I believe your landlady mentioned it."

"Oh yes, Mrs. Reach-Out-And-Touch. Do you want to know what she told me about you?" The gleam in his eyes switched from piercing to openly taunting.

"No, I don't," Sophie said stiffly. She could well imagine what he'd been told. The only way to defeat gossip was to deny its existence. At least that's what she'd been telling herself all these years.

"All right, so I go to the meeting of the town fathers," Fate said, getting back to the subject at hand. It wasn't like him to digress, but he was bushed. He'd been practically working around the clock ever since he'd got to town. And dammit, the woman brought out a streak of perverseness in him. Her Serene Highness. He'd been amused the first time he'd heard someone call her that.

"That's right. They meet every third Thursday at noon in the back room at Tom's Luncheonette. The meeting this Thursday will be about the landfill, cleaning up Dutchman's Creek, and the Dunwoody auction. It would be a good move on your part to accept the invitation, Mr. Ridgeway."

Neither of them bothered to mention just why it was so important for the representative of the New York firm that had taken over the town's single industry to walk softly and carry a big smile. In the process of getting things ready for the new management that would soon take over, Fate had necessarily stepped on a few toes.

"Is that the place with the barbecue?" he asked hopefully.

"The best," Sophie replied.

"Okay, I'll go then, but that doesn't mean I've agreed to take part in this damfool scheme."

"I understand, Mr. Ridgeway," Sophie said, rising smoothly and gathering her pencils and pad. If he insisted on dragging her into it, then perhaps she'd try to find a way to get him off the hook. The trouble was, she'd promised to deliver him, and Sophie never went back on a promise.

Back in her own office, she spent the remainder of the afternoon going over personnel files and scheduling appointments for the position of personnel director. The former personnel director, whose only qualification for the position had been his close relationship to the wife of a late chairman of the board, had been among the first to be "retired."

Buy the man indeed, she mused several hours later. She couldn't begin to count the men who'd offered to console her after her divorce. Most of them would probably have run hard the other way if she'd showed the slightest sign of taking them up on their offer. Sophie knew her strengths, but she also knew her weaknesses.

Ironically, her strength *was* her weakness. At least where men were concerned. It would almost be funny if it weren't so darned frustrating. She could just picture herself leaping about, waving dollar bills and screaming to outbid all the other women for a weekend with a particular bachelor. She'd perish on the spot. Either that or she'd start wheezing, the way she'd done as a child whenever she got upset or excited.

It was too much to hope that word wouldn't leak out. Early the next morning, Sophie was accosted before she got within two blocks of the office building. Shelly Peevy, a redheaded dynamo from shipping, gasped out the first question. "Sophie, I heard the boss is going to take part in the auction, and that he's set a five-thousand-dollar minimum and has the final say-so on who gets him, is that right?"

Sophie snorted. "If you're referring to Mr. Ridgeway, he hasn't even agreed yet to participate."

"Yeah, but he will, won't he?" asked a file clerk who'd hurried to catch up with them. "I mean, that's too much talent to go to waste. Talk about hunk city! How much do you think I could buy for twenty bucks?"

"For twenty bucks you get to touch the ground he walks on," Shelly quipped, and the two of them giggled. Sophie frowned.

By the end of the day, she was tempted to post progress reports on the bulletin board. It would have been easier than the constant interruptions. For reasons of her own, Sophie had always bent over backward to keep a low profile. She'd come in for enough speculation when she'd moved from Dunwoody into the community, and later on, living with FloBelle and Phil, and again when Phil had left her. She preferred to remain quietly in the background, but it wasn't always easy. At times like this it was downright impossible!

"Yes, Wendy, Mr. Ridgeway is considering taking part in the auction, but I'm fairly sure he isn't planning to offer a Hollywood screen test." A *screen test*?

"The tickets go on sale this weekend. They'll be ten dollars apiece, Susan, but I seriously doubt that it will be all that interesting."

Good cause or not, if she was going to be placed in the position of making a spectacle of herself, she didn't need the entire work force of KellyCo there as witnesses. She was going to have enough trouble going through with it without that.

Sophie had grown up in Turbyville. She'd been a Dunwoody product, having been left there by her mother when she was three. Turbyville was a fine, upstanding community, proud of its churches, its school, and its civic-mindedness. Even so, the townspeople were slow to grant approval to the "Dunwoody kids" as they termed them. Those who remained to become a part of the town always knew they were on probation until they'd proved themselves to be decent, hardworking citizens.

Sophie's road had been made more difficult by the fact that she'd been attractive. A real humdinger, the men had called her. Trouble, just you mark my words, women like Hester Kerner, Fate's landlady, had been fond of saying.

She'd made the grade, but it hadn't been easy. She'd learned to close her ears to lewd remarks and hide her long, blond hair, her slender, budding body, and the vulnerable expression that came from knowing herself alone and unprotected.

By the time she'd married Philip Pennybaker, she'd been exhausted with the effort of going to school nights, working days, helping out in the church nursery on Sundays, and trying to be so damned squeaky clean that the town couldn't help but approve of her.

Marriage was supposed to have solved everything. Phil had been fairly well respected, or so she'd thought at the time. Sophie had fully expected to share his reputation as a worthy citizen. They'd moved into the old River Street rental house with Phil's mother, FloBelle, because even with both of them working, it had been hard to make ends meet. Phil had been a sales rep for a pharmaceutical company, although not a very good one, despite the fact that he'd stayed on the road sometimes for days at a time.

Then one day he'd called from Augusta to tell her he'd met a widow with several small children who needed him far more than Sophie ever would, and he was going back to New Mexico with her. Sophie had had her hands full with her mother-in-law. FloBelle was something of a psychic, and she claimed her poor boy had been kidnapped by a bunch of foreigners and was being forced to eat the kind of food that always made his stomach act up.

Sophie had been almost relieved. Marriage had not turned out to be at all what she'd expected. She'd considered herself mature and levelheaded for an eighteen-year-old, but perhaps her hopes had been too high. Or perhaps what Phil had told her after years of trying to pretend everything was just lovely between them had been true: she was simply too strong for a woman. She intimidated a man. That hadn't been the precise term he'd used, but it was close enough. It was no wonder, he'd said, that he hadn't been able to perform. No man liked a woman who came on as strong as Sophie did.

Seek counseling, the syndicated columnists had advised. From whom? Where? There was no one in Turbyville Sophie could trust with a devastating secret like that. Instead, she'd settled for companionship, and tried harder. Phil had never been unkind. He was really a very gentle man, and all in all, they'd had a reasonably nice marriage. Or so she'd thought.

Phil had eventually married his widow with her five children. He'd kept the car and Sophie had kept Flo-Belle. Her security had never been seriously threatened—at least not her financial security.

Well, she'd lived through all that, she reminded herself. The affairs of the Pennybakers had kept the town amused all one steamy summer. She'd survived Dunwoody, desertion and divorce, along with all the attendant gossip. She certainly should be able to get through a small thing like a charity auction.

* * *

"Come on, Sophie, he's *gotta* do it," Sherry said, falling in beside her as they walked through the main gates the following morning. "It's the most exciting thing that's happened since the one last year, but when it comes to bachelors, this town's scraping the bottom of the barrel and everybody knows it."

"I'm still working on him. I expect he'll fall in line," Sophie said with a smile that was less serene than smug. "He ought to bring in enough to remodel the cafeteria, at least. The counter's so high the big kids have to lift the little kids up so they can reach the food."

"That's right, you're a Dunwoody alumnus, aren't you? I'd almost forgotten."

"Thanks," said Sophie, and they both knew what she meant. "It's pretty well in the bag."

It wasn't. "God, how did I manage to get involved in this business," Fate Ridgeway fumed without looking up from his cluttered desk. "Some barracuda from the local newspaper tackled me in the parking lot, and I practically had to throttle her to get away."

Sophie, pad in hand, waited quietly. She prided herself on the fact that no hint of what she was feeling was visible on her face. She knew very well that there wasn't a hair out of place in the neat beige coil at the back of her head, and as always when she was at work, her clothes were modest, becoming, and unobtrusive.

"She probably wanted to know what you'll be offering. Shall I write up a brief statement for the press?"

Fate's response was short and to the point. Actually Sophie was rather interested herself. Like it or not, it seemed that she'd be on the receiving end of whatever date package her employer put together. A weekend with L. Fate Ridgeway, she mused, concealing the thrill of excitement that coursed through her.

Stupid! Of course, she wouldn't actually win him. He was the *pièce de résistance* of the whole affair. All the same, the thought of slinging him over her shoulder and walking off into the night brought on a feeling not unlike those Phil used to complain of after she'd tried out one of her more creative recipes on him. Phil was a meat-and-potatoes man. Fried and mashed, respectively.

"Have you decided yet?" she asked when she considered the silence had extended far enough. She had work to do, even if Lafayette Ridgeway had nothing better to do than sit and scowl.

"Decided what? Oh—the auction thing." The scowl deepened, and Sophie darted a quick look at his eyes. The color always fascinated her. It was the color of the pines in her backyard on a cloudy day, a sort of muted, opaque green.

Fate interrupted her muddled daydream. "You want a statement for the press? I'll give you one. I'm offering a month in traction to the next reporter who wastes my time with damfool questions."

Sophie's irritation showed itself only in the faint compression of her lips. "For your information, Mr. Ridgeway, the county spends more than twice as much on its jails as it does on the Dunwoody children."

The chrome-and-leather chair squeaked, and Fate's arms came down on the desk, his scowl deepening. "What if I offered to pay ten thousand dollars to let me off the hook?"

A small gasp escaped her. "Ten thousand—" she repeated faintly.

"Just get my name off that list, and I'll write out a check this minute." He ran a finger inside his collar, and Sophie noticed a faint film of moisture on his brow.

Her well-groomed eyebrows lifted in surprise. KellyCo's acting CEO—which stood for Chief Execution Official, according to the plant scuttlebutt—was *nervous*? The head hatchet man sent down here to weed out this antiquated, nepotism-ridden old stack of bricks and machinery, was actually squirming?

Sophie decided then and there that even if she had to suffer for it, she wasn't going to let him off so easily. "An affair of this sort is possible only when it has the enthusiastic support of the whole community," she informed him. "If you back out, the other bachelors will, too. As a group, they're perfectly willing to go along, but individually, they probably feel too self-conscious."

"Self-conscious!" he roared, looking every bit as dangerous and predatory as he was reputed to be. "Does a side of prime beef feel self-conscious hanging in the meat locker?"

Prime? The man had a pretty high opinion of himself, didn't he? Still, in all fairness she was forced to admit he was probably entitled. While he might not win any popularity contests among the employees who'd had to clean up their act, when it came to a question of masculine pulchritude, Fate Ridgeway won hands down.

"Yes, um—as I was saying..." What *had* she been saying? More importantly, what had *he* been saying?

"All right, Mrs. Pennybaker, public relations has never been one of my long suits—" Sophie almost strangled on that one "—but I value your opinions, and if you think it's important, then I suppose I can bring myself to go through with it. Whatever happened to the good old charity balls and fund-raising dinners, where all a man had to contend with was cold food and uncomfortable clothes?"

"We don't do things that way in Turbyville," she said primly. Inside she was jubilant. She could almost find it in her heart to feel sorry for the man, but his participation would guarantee the success of the whole venture.

"There's not a lot to do for entertainment around here, as you might have noticed. The fire department sponsors an all-day barbecue with country music, and the school puts on carnivals and plays, but other than a movie theater, church socials, and a private club or two, people pretty much make their own fun."

"How long do you think this affair will last?"

"I have no idea. I understand it's not absolutely necessary for you to be present for the actual auction if there's a conflict." *If you'd rather stay home and hide under the bed.* "The bachelors do videos, you see, and then the videos are shown on a large screen throughout the evening. I understand last year when the March of Dimes did a bachelor auction, the actual bidding didn't start until ten."

"Thus prolonging the agony."

"That's one point of view. I've heard that a few of the—uh, participants declined to attend in person."

"I can imagine," Fate said dryly. The crease in his left cheek deepened as his lips twisted into a parody of a smile.

"You might enjoy it. There'll be champagne and a band. I understand it's all very festive."

"You've never attended?" His eyes echoed the mockery of his smile.

"No." Sophie didn't elaborate. Her private life was none of his business, and his was none of hers. She preferred to keep it that way. She had enough trouble thinking of him as merely an employer, and a temporary one, at that. If she let herself start speculating about his personal life, she'd never get anything accomplished. It was important to remember that she'd be here long after he'd gone back to New York, or wherever Bannerman needed him next.

Several hours later Fate shoved aside the report he'd been working on and swiveled his chair around to stare unseeingly out the window. Interesting woman, Sophie Pennybaker. Irritating, but...interesting. The first time he'd laid eyes on her, he'd thought she was completely devoid of personality.

Then he'd taken a second look.

What was it they called her around the plant, Her Serene Highness? He was beginning to understand how she'd earned the title. She was about as capable a woman as he'd ever worked with. He'd come in here cold and started turning things upside down, and she'd never raised an eyebrow, much less her voice. Raised a few temperatures, probably—including his—not that she did it deliberately. If anything, she played down her attributes. It had been weeks before he'd discovered that she had a damned fine build under those jacket things she wore.

He sighed. Toying with a pencil, he stared out the window at the view of roofs, steeples, and treetops. His office was on the top floor of the town's only skyscraper, all of five stories high. It had been built about sixty years ago, expensively overdecorated by the last management, and was so ugly it was almost appealing.

He watched the rush-hour traffic for a few minutes—it only took a few minutes to clear out—and then his thoughts turned back to Sophie. An unusual woman, his secretary. Something about her bothered him, but damned if he could put his finger on it. She was *too* good, maybe that was it. He knew for a fact that she was only thirty-three years old, yet she acted like a woman twice that age. There were times—not many, but a few—when she looked up a certain way, and he could've sworn she was a young, inexperienced girl.

Hell, she didn't even wear makeup, or if she did, it wasn't noticeable. No nail polish. Her fingers were ringless, her hands small, firm, and nicely shaped. It was her eyes he liked most, Fate decided. They were pure gray. Not blue, not hazel, but gray. She had a way of looking at him that was so direct he sometimes lost his train of thought, and as far as he could tell, she didn't use any of that stuff women put on their lashes that made them look like sleepy raccoons when they woke up in his bed the morning after.

Not that any woman had woken up in his bed in a long time.

And that was another problem. How the devil was a man supposed to manage his private life when he rented a single room from a woman so nosey she dusted off the shirts hanging in his closet?

As the days passed and the auction drew nearer, Fate grew more irritable, Sophie more quiet. She'd come to terms with her own role in the affair. She'd handle it the same way she'd always handled the crises in her life.

Well—not with an attack of the wheezies. She hadn't had one of those since her best friend, Eloise had gotten adopted and gone off to live in West Virginia. Sophie, who'd been eleven then, had seen friend after friend taken away from her. She'd been furious. She'd stolen Eloise's lace-trimmed socks and promptly lapsed into an attack of asthma that had lasted for days, but she'd finally learned not to make attachments, and she hadn't. Not until she'd married Phil and FloBelle. By the time that particular attachment had come undone, she'd discovered that she was quite capable of doing without close attachments. She had FloBelle for company when she needed someone, and she had a good, if not exciting job, with a decent retirement plan.

The taping session was scheduled, and still Sophie had been told nothing of what Fate planned for his date package. It was a question she was asked several times a day. "It's going to be a surprise," was her stock answer. She refused to risk her ears by asking him. His temper was so short these days she occasionally wondered if he was trying to get her to give up and let him off the hook.

Fat chance, Lafayette, she thought with malicious satisfaction. I was born tougher than you'll ever be!

Fate brooded. The woman was getting to him with that sphinx act of hers. Twice in one day when he'd misplaced some important papers, he'd bitten her head off, and it had rolled off her like water off a duck's back. She'd found the papers where he'd shoved them and brought him a sandwich, a glass of milk, and two aspirin.

He'd already checked out her personnel file and found it distinctly unsatisfying. She'd been with the company sixteen years, starting as a typist. She'd completed several courses in business, evidently at night, as there was no indication of her having taken a leave of absence. She was divorced.

There was nothing at all to explain why a woman with her capabilities should be stuck here in a slack-water town, where hosing down the new fire truck was a crowd-gathering event. She could have gone to Columbia, or Augusta—or even Atlanta or Charlotte. Hell, she could've gone anywhere and made it. Her pay was adequate, but she could have doubled it in the same job in New York.

Of course, her living expenses would also double, as well as her stress load. Maybe she knew when she was well-off; who was he to say? He was no shining example. He'd let himself get talked out of what he'd really wanted to do, and by the time he'd had any serious second thoughts, it was too late. He'd had too much time and money invested in preparing him for the wrong career.

The taping was scheduled for two o'clock on Monday, the auction set for the following Friday night, and Fate was definitely in. The clerical staff at KellyCo's was at fever pitch. L. L. Ridgeway had developed almost as big a fan club among the men, who recognized what he'd done for the future of KellyCo, as he had among the women, who admired him for a slightly different reason.

"What's he like in private, Sophie?"

"In his private office, you mean? Very much like he is anywhere else, I should imagine. Extremely efficient."

"Oh, c'mon, you can tell us, Sophie. We passed his test—we're all home safe."

Sophie knew about the test. She'd personally ushered scores of salaried employees into that leather-paneled office during the first two weeks and seen them emerge again a few minutes later, wiping the perspiration from their brows. Fate had given each of them five minutes to justify their paycheck. To their credit, most of them had passed. Of those who had not, some had been given a second chance, others had been relocated. A few had chosen early retirement, but except for the handful who'd been fired for dishonesty, all those let go had been given generous separation packages.

Sophie continued to field all the questions with her usual skill. Just after eleven on Monday she slipped into Fate's office with a stack of letters for his signature. He was turned toward the window, scowling out at the water tower.

Had the man been born with a scowl on his face? she wondered. At some time in his life, surely he must've found *something* to smile about. If he had any idea what a difference it made, he might try it more often. "The video people will be here at two-thirty, Mr. Ridgeway. Where would you prefer the taping take place?"

"Approximately five thousand miles from wherever I happen to be, Mrs. Pennybaker."

Sophie's lips tightened perceptibly. The man was a poor loser. Somehow, she'd have expected him to be more graceful about it. "I should've thought of this before, but if you'd care to view a few of the tapes from last year's March of Dimes auction, I think I can arrange it. It might give you an idea of what's appropriate."

Leaning back in his chair, Fate closed his eyes, and it occurred to Sophie that a man in his position must be under incredible pressure. She felt an unexpected surge of tenderness that would have horrified him if he'd known about it. It rather terrified her.

"Suppose you just summarize, Mrs. Pennybaker," he said tiredly. His eyes remained closed.

"I didn't actually see any of the others, you understand, but I believe the men involved told a little about themselves first, their interests and their preferences in a date. Then they went on to describe their proposition, making it sound as attractive as possible."

His left cheek creased, and he opened his eyes, sending her a look that made her feel uncomfortably warm. "Go on, Mrs. Pennybaker. I'm to make my proposition sound attractive. Then what?"

He was doing it deliberately, Sophie thought, grinding her molars. He knew darned well she didn't like this business any more than he did, and he was making her pay for having got them both involved in it. Her head came up the fraction necessary so that she appeared to be looking down her nose at him. "It might help you to know what some of the men offered last year," she said calmly. "I believe one of them gave a weekend cruise to Nassau, and another one a shopping spree in Paris. With a limit, of course."

"Of course," he repeated, his face grave.

"Yes, well—most of the dates are weekend affairs— New York and a Broadway show, or a ski trip, or maybe golf and tennis at some nice resort. The men try to offer a date package that will attract a high-dollar bid. That's their contribution." She gradually became aware of the fact that her fingers were pinching tiny pleats in her skirt, and surreptitiously brushed them out. "The women's donation is whatever amount they're willing to bid for a date with a particular man."

He studied her silently for what seemed hours. Sophie resisted the impulse to fill that silence with words. If he thought he could discomfit her, he was sadly mistaken. She'd ridden out far worse storms than L. Lafayette Ridgeway and survived.

"I get the picture," he said finally. "In other words, the men give the women whatever they can afford, and the women take whatever the men are willing to offer. What do the poor orphans get out of all this, if you don't mind my asking?"

"The poor orphans, as you call them," Sophie snapped, having overestimated her forbearance, "get every cent the women pay for the dubious privilege of the men's company, *plus* the money raised by selling tickets! The club donates the ballroom and all refreshments, the video company donates their services, and even the publicity is free! Every newspaper in the area will be covering the affair, raising public awareness about the deplorable conditions at Dunwoody Farm and bringing in still more donations. Does that satisfy you?"

"I wonder why it hasn't been tried on the national debt?" Fate asked mildly. Raising one shirtsleeved arm, he kneaded the muscles at the back of his neck, and Sophie drew in a deep, steadying breath.

What on earth had got into her? She hadn't blown up this way since—well, in years. "Being a newcomer, you may not know about the Dunwoody Farm, but it's a private institution, Mr. Ridgeway. It was supported entirely from a trust fund until fairly recently, but the trust had evidently been poorly handled, and well...the money just ran out. The whole place has been deteriorating for as long as I can remember. Some of the buildings should've been condemned years ago, but there was nowhere for the children to go, so the authorities just looked the other way and hoped for the best. Now the town's been given a year to get them back in shape. The buildings, I mean—not the children," she added hastily.

"I know what you mean, Mrs. Pennybaker."

"Yes, well...so you can see why it's important. To raise enough money, I mean. And people don't always respond to a letter asking for funds. They get so many these days, for every cause imaginable."

"And a few that aren't."

Once more Sophie found her attention straying along totally irrelevant lines. Unlike so many of his predecessors, Fate Ridgeway didn't depend on custom-tailored suits and handmade shirts to lend him an air of authority. His tie was askew, and his cuffs were usually turned back within half an hour of his arrival at the office. Nevertheless, the aura of command he exuded was an almost palpable force.

"All right, Mrs. Pennybaker, I gave my word," he said tiredly, breaking into her thoughts. "We're going to do it, but as I said before, we'll do it my way." A wicked gleam appeared in his eyes. "I'll do the video, you'll attend the auction and buy my services, and then

I'll write out a check and we'll both forget the whole thing and get back to business, all right?"

Sophie shifted uneasily. Forget the whole thing? Did that mean she wasn't going anywhere? All that agony and she didn't even get a two-day trip out of it?

Actually, the last thing she wanted was to go off on a trip with Lafayette Ridgeway, but it would've been nice to have been offered the option. "That could be considered bid rigging, couldn't it?"

"The intent was never to profit by deceit, Mrs. Pennybaker. Your orphans will get every cent of the money. In fact, I'll write out a check right now for the amount we agreed on if that will placate your puritanical little conscience. I doubt that any woman's going to bid more than ten bucks for my package, anyway, so I think we're being more than fair here, don't you?"

Ten bucks? Either the man was a fool or he was fishing for compliments. As either choice was highly unlikely, Sophie could only assume he intended to cover himself completely with a sheet.

"I think it would be better to wait until after the auction like everyone else, Mr. Ridgeway," Sophie said stiffly.

"Whatever you say, Mrs. P."

She left with the sound of a low chuckle ringing in her ears.

Two

Sophie smelled the incense even before she opened the door. It was a good thing she'd called earlier and reminded FloBelle to put the chicken on to stew. Sophie had gotten it ready before she'd left for work that morning, as she didn't quite trust her mother-in-law's taste in herbs. The comfrey in the baked fish last week had definitely been a loser.

"Hello-o, I'm home," she called through the screen door. Her jacket was off by the time she got as far as the hall, her belt a moment later. Only then did she allow her shoulders to sag, thankful she could drop all pretense at looking calm, cool and collected. After a day like this one had been, she'd settle for looking marginally intelligent, never mind the extras.

"Sophie, you look plumb frazzled out," accused the small round woman who drifted into the room with a battered-looking book in her hand. "Your aura's the color of dirty burlap. Why don't you come lie in my parlor a little while and let the pink work on you?"

"Maybe later," Sophie said gently. FloBelle firmly believed that different colors radiated different types of energy. She'd painted her living quarters a rather startling shade of Pepto Bismol pink, and while Sophie didn't discount the theory, she didn't exactly endorse it, either. Just to be on the safe side she'd chosen white for her own rooms on the second floor.

"Then I'll turn my music up so you can enjoy it while you change, all right? It'll help you relax."

"That'll be lovely, Flo." With earplugs it would be lovely. There was no possible way Sophie could explain that she greatly preferred to relax to the sound of silence and the random muted tones of her wind chimes. Not for the world would she do anything to hurt her friend's feelings. There were times when looking after a slightly flaky fifty-nine-year-old semipsychic demanded the last shred of her patience, but she always seemed to manage somehow.

FloBelle was unique in a town with more than its share of eccentrics. She still wore her long hair in a braid down her back, often with blossoms woven among its iron-gray strands, and her clothes were a combination of early flower-child and leftover Halloween. Unique. That was the word Sophie used to describe her mother-in-law. A little strange, but oddly endearing.

"Did you find out when Mr. Ridgeway was born?"

The disposition of a saint, the guilelessness of a child, Sophie continued in her silent assessment—and the persistence of an IRS agent. "No, I did *not* find out when Mr. Ridgeway was born. Would you please back off? He's my boss, that's all, and even that's purely temporary."

"For weeks now, the queen of diamonds has been right smack dab against the king of spades, and both of them have been surrounded by high hearts. I'm telling you, honey, the cards don't lie. Somebody's hovering on the brink."

"Me!" Sophie snapped. "I'm hovering on the brink of starvation. Did you turn the chicken down once it came to a boil?"

FloBelle's brow puckered in concentration. A real whiz at dealing with vague theories and hazy concepts, she was never at her best when confronted with hard facts. The phrases "I feel" and "I believe" cropped up frequently in her conversations. Never, in the fifteen years Sophie had known her, had FloBelle Pennybaker begun a single statement with the words, "I think."

Meanwhile, the sitars and bamboo flutes in the next room wailed relentlessly.

"The chicken and vegetables in the stewpot, remember, Flo? You were supposed to put it on so it would be done by dinnertime."

"I remember you called," Flo said thoughtfully. "I feel almost certain I did what you said, only Ramu was here this afternoon, and we got to talking, and I can't seem to remember now if it ever boiled or not."

Ramu, as nearly as Sophie could make out, had been dead some twenty-two hundred years. Flo called him her spirit guide, and depended on him for everything from weather reports to home remedies. Lately, Ramu had been urging her to move to some town in Arizona. Sophie was beginning to suspect him of being in cahoots with the chamber of commerce.

"I'd better go see," she said tiredly, fairly certain of what she'd find.

Some forty-five minutes later Sophie finished the last of her broiled cheese-and-tomato sandwich, wiped off the table and rinsed out the two iced-tea glasses. The chicken simmered on the stove; they'd have it tomorrow. One of these days she'd learn that if she wanted the stove turned on, she'd have to say so. She'd asked FloBelle to put the chicken on, and that was precisely what she'd done.

It was just that sort of thing that had convinced Sophie that her mother-in-law needed someone to look after her after Phil had left. The world wasn't safe for a woman whose mind was usually tuned to a different frequency. To put it mildly.

Besides, she enjoyed living with her for the most part. After all these years there was a deep bond of affection between the two women that bridged any differences in age, temperament or background. Not that Sophie knew what her own background was.

She knew her name, her age, and her birthday. She'd been able to guess from things she'd heard that her mother had been young and probably unmarried. Smith might not even be her real surname, but at least the Pennybaker part was legal. That was one of the reasons she'd kept Phil's name after the divorce.

When she thought about herself at all, Sophie considered herself a self-made woman. Considering the raw material she'd had to work with, she was quite proud of what she'd been able to accomplish. She'd had health problems as a child. Inclined to be rebellious, she was usually in trouble with the cottage mother for some infraction or another.

The asthma had come on unexpectedly, and it had been terrifying. It had been years since she'd suffered an attack, but she could still remember the sensation of being suffocated. Panic had only made matters worse. The visiting nurse and doctor had tried various medications, none of which had worked very well. Some of them had made her even sicker. Her cottage mother had been encouraged to let her "tough it out," which had suited Sophie just fine.

In fact, toughing it out had been the beginning of what she liked to think of as her reconstruction period. The first few times she'd heard someone say it was all in her head when she'd been gasping for breath, she'd thought they simply didn't understand what was happening to her. She'd tried to explain. After a while she'd come to believe that they must be right. In which case, it would go away if she could only concentrate hard enough.

She'd avoided the visiting nurse like the plague and concentrated on learning to concentrate. When her good friend, Minnie Lee, was adopted, Sophie had wheezed, but she hadn't gasped or turned blue. By the time Barbara Pettigrew's parents had patched things up enough to take her back home with them, Sophie had scarcely even breathed hard.

Eloise had been the last hurdle. She'd let herself believe that one day, someone would want a pair of eleven-year-old girls enough to go to the trouble of tracking down Sophie's mother and getting permission to adopt her, and then she and Eloise would be sisters.

It hadn't happened. When Eloise had left Dunwoody, Sophie hadn't handled it well at all, but it had finally showed her what she had to do. She'd be safe as long as she didn't count on anyone for anything.

She'd learned. By the time she was in high school, she'd learned two more things about herself. She was attractive to boys, and she had a quick mind. Along with courses in everything from library science and Latin, to typing and technical writing, she'd attended the obligatory classes in sex education. They'd called it something else, of course—girl's hygiene. But the message had been plain enough; boys only want one thing from a girl, and if she gives it to them, her name will be written on the wall of every phone booth and men's room from Turbyville to Monck's Corner.

As a deterrent, it was extremely effective. Sophie was reasonably certain that her name had never graced a single wall, not even the ladies' room at the Center Theater, which had always been a regular who's who of Turbyville's courting couples.

When she was seventeen, living in a single room on River Street with a widow, she met Phil Pennybaker, who lived next door with his mother, and for the first and only time in her life, Sophie fell in love. At eighteen, she'd married herself a family and considered herself the luckiest woman in the world.

At eighteen she'd been incredibly stupid.

"I've invited some people over Friday night for psychometry," FloBelle announced when Sophie came downstairs the next morning. "Why don't you join us. You could bring home something from the office, maybe Mr. Ridgeway's pen or pencil. Essie's getting real good. Last week she meditated on Shuford Peebles's pocket comb and told him what kind of car his grandson drove, right down to the bumper sticker."

"Oh, goodness, there's no telling what a person could do with that kind of information," Sophie teased. "Thanks, Flo, but I've already made plans for Friday night."

Flo's round blue eyes sparkled like dime-store sapphires. "You're going out? Does that mean you have a date?"

"Nope."

"You're going out alone? Where?"

Sophie was sorry she'd said anything at all. Taking her keys out of her bag, she dropped them into the dusty apron of Flo's gilded Buddha. "I'm walking today, so if you need to go anywhere, take the car."

She might've known bribery wouldn't work. "Sophie, are you by any chance going to that male sale thing they're puttin' on for the Dunwoody children?"

"Not by any chance," Sophie replied dryly. "By sheer coercion. My boss wants me there."

"Oo-hoo-ooo," FloBelle crooned, sounding more like an owl than a woman bent on extracting the last morsel of information about a subject dear to her heart—romance.

"You can just get that bird-dog look off your face, FloBelle Pennybaker, there's absolutely no chance of anything like that. I happen to work for the man, that's all," Sophie said firmly.

"Of course you do, honey. So is he taking you to this thing? Does he call you by your given name yet? You forgot to tell me when he was born—oh, and could you find out where, and what time of day, too?"

"Flo—" Sophie backed out the front door, laughing.

"Notice what his thumbs look like, Sophie," the older woman called after her. "In fact, if you could get a handprint—"

"I'll stop by the sheriff's office and see if they have anything on file. FloBelle, you're awful! Stop trying to marry me off to some plastic playing card, I'm perfectly happy the way I am."

She headed toward town, knowing full well that FloBelle would be hounding her until she brought home his head on a platter—or at least a chunk of his hair. As if anything could be gleaned from a few strands of soft, sooty black hair with random threads of silver. Heaven help her if Flo ever discovered that Leonidas Lafayette Ridgeway was called Fate by his closest associates. Sophie would have to quit her job and leave town!

Thursday. The day before the auction. Sophie read Petra George's column over coffee and grunted her disapproval.

> It's not exactly a marriage bureau, folks, and the committee that dreamed up Turbyville's latest fund-raiser insists it's all good clean fun in the name of sweet charity, but if it walks like a marriage bureau and it talks like a marriage bureau, then chances are it's not a duck. Just between us, did you know that three of the couples who went on last year's auction dates came back engaged? And two of those were ones that took along another couple as chaperons!

> Count on us to stay on top of the situation as it develops, Turbyvillains and villainesses. If we see any signs of puncture wounds that look as if they might have been made by Cupid's dart, you'll be the first to know.

"Trash!" Sophie grumbled. "Utter drivel!" She flung the paper aside. With her nervous energy running at an all-time high, she'd been turning out prodigious amounts of work all week, but she'd been sleeping badly and waking increasingly early, unable to go back to sleep. Irritated at letting this whole business get under her skin, she stomped back upstairs, gathered up the underwear she'd worn the day before, and threw it into the bathtub. Then she adjusted the shower and stepped under the sharp spray.

Lathering herself, and muttering under her breath, she automatically trod on her clothes, turning them with her toe so that the sudsy water pounded down on them until she was finished with her bath. With typical efficiency, Sophie had reasoned long ago that if laundry could be done with rocks and sticks and muddy river water, it could just as effectively be done with feet, soap and a porcelain tub. And with a lot less energy.

The sun was barely splintering through the tops of the pine trees by the time she'd covered the mile and a quarter to work, and already she was wringing wet. There'd been thunderstorms hanging about for days now; it was that time of year. Thundery weather always made her feel edgy. Not scared, just restless. Unsettled. As if something momentous were creeping up on her.

It didn't help later on that afternoon when she got back from lunch, hearing the talk in the ladies' lounge. She was standing in front of a mirror, trying to counteract the effects of humidity on her normally smooth hairstyle.

"—the way his mouth sorta tilts to the left when he smiles," came a voice from one stall.

"Smiles! When did he ever smile at you? He's got Her Serene Highness standing by in case he ever feels like smiling."

"Okay, so when he sneers. What's the difference? It uses all the same muscles."

"Yeah, the same ones he uses for kissing," a voice at the end of the row said dreamily, and then there was a chorus of giggles.

Frowning, Sophie jabbed a hairpin into her scalp. Tidy or not, she'd had just about all she could take from the Fate Ridgeway fan club. One more word and she was going to let out a shriek that would rival the noon whistle! Tucking in her shirttail, she smoothed her skirt, patted her hair one last time, and grimaced at her reflection. Good enough. She might be boiling on the inside, but she'd pass inspection. She'd always found a cool head and a flawless appearance the best defense against... whatever.

But head and appearance notwithstanding, there was no defending herself against the incessant speculation. Before she'd even settled back behind her desk, one of the typists poked her head through the door to ask if Sophie knew what sort of date package L.L. was planning to offer some lucky woman.

Sophie looked pointedly at her watch. "Melia, it's a quarter of three. Have you finished your work already?"

The bouncy little blonde grinned impishly. "They had us matching shade samples, and I had to wash my hands, so I thought I'd just pop in and see if you knew. Some of us are thinking about going shares on him. I've got sixty-seven dollars, and since it was my idea, I've got dibs on his lips. One kiss," she said, closing her eyes in anticipated ecstasy. "One wet, wild, wicked kiss to dream on, that's all I'm asking."

"I thought you were engaged."

"I am, but just because a woman's on a diet, that doesn't mean she can't give in to temptation now and then. And that man is temptation on the hoof."

Susan Ponder, her brown eyes sparkling behind oversize glasses, came down the hall from the ladies' lounge and lingered to put in her two cents' worth. "Honey, I'd trade all the peach cobblers in the world for a slice of that," she said with a sigh. "A lean, mean, lovin' machine. Are you going to bid on him, Sophie?" She cast a wickedly teasing look at Sophie and darted out.

Sophie wiped the damp palms of her hands with a crumpled square of embroidered linen and tucked it into the breast pocket of her tailored white blouse. The crisp two-piece outfit had been comfortable enough this morning when she'd come to work, and the new air-conditioning system was superefficient. But she dreaded the walk home. She'd be poached before she ever got there.

By five-thirty the building was all but empty. Fate had gone out just before four and hadn't come back. Sophie assumed he was gone for the day. She'd finished proofing the letters she'd typed earlier and frowned at a set of figures. She'd better double-check the data just to be sure.

"Hi, Miz Pennybaker, 'bye Miz Pennybaker!"

Sophie, bent over a file cabinet, glanced over her shoulders to see Wendy, one of her favorites among the production order clerks. Like Sophie, Wendy had gone to work right out of high school. Unlike Sophie, she'd made no effort at all to change her image, at least not until Sophie had tactfully pointed out that tight blue jeans, cutout tops, and masses of long, curly hair, really weren't all that suitable if a woman wanted to get ahead in the business world. "Good night, Wendy. By the way, I really like your new hairstyle," she added.

"Thanks, Miz P. My boyfriend says it makes me look intelligent." The small face suddenly clouded with uncertainty. "I wonder if he meant that as a compliment?"

"I'm sure he did, Wendy."

Smiling, Sophie returned to her search. With everyone gone, perhaps she could have a few minutes of peace and quiet to do a little more organizing in her files. She wasn't all that anxious to walk home with it still broiling hot outside. There was nothing on TV she particularly wanted to see tonight, but maybe she'd leave in time to stop by Harnett's Drugstore on the way home and pick up a brand-new paperback instead of borrowing another one of Flo's endless supply of secondhand books. Goodness knows she needed something to help her to relax. The muscles of her back were so knotted up she probably creaked every time she changed position.

A few minutes later she absently unbuttoned the top buttons of her blouse and adjusted a slip strap with one hand as she pulled out the next drawer down. Whatever she wanted was invariably in a bottom drawer somewhere. One of these days she'd finish getting all the data transferred to the computer, but until that happened, she always double-checked everything. The last CEO had thought redecorating his office more important than bringing the computer system up-to-date. The half of it that wasn't obsolete was still incomplete, which just meant double the work for all concerned.

She felt a run start at her knee and swore softly. Peering over to see if it had gone too far to stop, she felt her hair catch in the brass pull on the next drawer up, and yanked it free, leaving behind several pale, gleaming strands. She swore again.

Starting with that wretched little piece in the *Turbyville Times*, it had turned out to be another one of those days. She'd be glad when the blasted auction was over. Then maybe she could relax again.

Thank goodness she'd had the foresight to make potato salad and fry a chicken this morning before she'd left the house. She was in no mood to cook now, and besides, it was too hot to heat up the kitchen at this late hour.

She bent over again, and her ornamental buckle cut into her stomach. Unsnapping her belt, Sophie allowed it to dangle from the loops on her skirt. Back at her desk a few minutes later, she slipped off a shoe and wriggled her toes. It felt so good, she removed the other one, pressing both feet against the slick surface of her vinyl antistatic mat.

Nibbling on her bottom lip, she checked the hard copy from the file against the version on her computer screen. They were identical, and she made a tiny pencil check at the top of the page. One more loose end taken care of—only a few thousand more to go. Meanwhile, if she wanted any of her own fried chicken, she'd best get home. FloBelle had been known to clean out the whole refrigerator after an evening of vigorous communing.

Replacing the file, Sophie wriggled her shoulders in an effort to rid herself of accumulated tension. Maybe she'd take her own supper out on her upstairs porch and watch the heat lightning over in the west. Thunder had been rumbling all afternoon, but the weatherman on the noon report had explained in laborious detail why it couldn't possibly rain.

Fried chicken, a brand-new thriller, and enough breeze to stir an occasional tinkle from her wind chimes. Now that sounded like a perfect antidote for what ailed her. Covering a yawn, she stretched, and then, impulsively, bent over from the waist, belt ends drooping, elbows flapping, fingers wriggling over her stockinged toes, feeling an almost pleasurable pain in the stiff muscles of her back. Not even the thought of the auction was going to keep her from sleeping tonight.

Still wriggling and flapping, Sophie gradually sensed that she was no longer alone. Bottoms up, she froze.

The cleaning crew. Let it be one of the cleaning crew, please Lord, because they didn't know her from Adam.

"Lost a contact, Mrs. Pennybaker?" Fate Ridgeway inquired from the doorway.

Sophie closed her twenty-twenty eyes and considered lying. It still wouldn't explain the unfastened belt, the untidy hair, the bare feet, or the shirttail that had slipped its moorings with all her bending and stretching.

Or her red face.

Moving as deliberately as if she were balancing a water jug on her head, she straightened and crossed to her desk. She buckled her belt and felt about for her shoes. "No, Mr. Ridgeway, I didn't lose a contact. I get stiff after sitting in one position for too long, that's all. If you don't need me for anything else, I'll be leaving now."

"Does it help, Sophie?"

Startled, she looked directly into his face, and then regretted it. He looked... different tonight. Tired, yes, but that was nothing new. They'd both been working like Trojans ever since he'd gotten here. It was common knowledge that the lights in his office often burned far into the night, and he was usually at work long before anyone else. In a town like Turbyville, where the same few families had lived and spawned since the first D'Urberville had come up the Congaree with the law on his tail, there were very few secrets.

"Does what help?" she asked, startled at the husky sound of her own voice. He'd never called her Sophie before. It was a small thing; Mr. Potter had always called her Sophie, but somehow, it sounded different coming from Fate Ridgeway.

"That. What you were doing."

"Stretching, you mean. Yes, I suppose so."

Fate leaned his shoulders against the doorframe, still feeling shaken by his unexpected reaction to seeing her flushed and untidy, as if she'd just been well kissed—or thoroughly tumbled in a bed. He must be even more bushed than he'd thought if the sight of a tousled Sophie could send every hormone in his body racing to battle stations.

He waited until he thought he could speak without sounding like a crack-voiced adolescent. "Mind if I call you Sophie from now on?"

"Actually, I prefer being called Mrs. Pennybaker."

Levering himself away from the door, Fate crossed to one of the two comfortable visitors' chairs and sat down, tossing his jacket across the glass topped coffee table. His shirt was unbuttoned at the neck and turned back at the cuffs; the silk and worsted tie he'd crammed into the pocket hours before began slithering onto the floor. He ignored it. Crossing his arms behind his head, he unconsciously flexed his muscles to ease their tension. "I think I prefer Sophie, Your Serene Highness." One lean cheek creased in the threat of a smile.

Sophie's lips tightened. So he'd heard that silly title. She might have known nothing would escape his attention, not even trivia. What else had he heard about her? Not that she particularly cared. "Mr. Ridgeway, I'm sure you'll call me whatever you want to call me, with or without my permission."

"What did Potter call you?"

"He called me Sophie, of course." Sophie was still standing beside her desk, trying not to gaze down at the compellingly masculine figure sprawled untidily across one of her chairs.

"Why of course?"

"Why—? Well, because he was old enough to be my grandfather, I suppose. And I wasn't Mrs. Pennybaker when I first came to work at KellyCo."

"I'm not old enough to be your grandfather, Sophie Smith Pennybaker, but I think I'll call you Sophie anyway. Which *doesn't* give you the privilege of calling me Leonidas," he tacked on with another of those mocking grins that affected her so strangely. "Your car wasn't in the parking lot. Did you walk this morning?"

She nodded.

"It's raining. I'll run you home."

"I have an umbrella."

"It's also blowing. Now don't be tedious, Sophie. Get your things, okay?"

One of the reasons she'd come as far as she had at KellyCo was that Sophie had learned early when arguing would help and when it was a waste of time. Besides, the thought of walking a mile and a quarter in the blowing rain didn't really appeal to her.

The car he drove was not unlike the man himself, lean, dark, with an understated aura of power she suspected could be intimidating under the right circumstances. Sophie fastened her seat belt and cut a quick look at his profile as he drove under the lights and exited the parking lot. She, of course, was not intimidated. Nor even impressed. At least no more than any normal woman would be impressed by an attractive, intelligent, and obviously virile man.

In a tight little voice, she directed him to the two-story frame house on River Street. There were only four, and theirs was the last one, plopped down in the middle of several acres of woods and overgrown fields.

Neither of them spoke, but Sophie was acutely aware of him—of the faint clean fragrance of his after-shave mingled with the warm scent of masculine flesh. It was the weather, of course. Thunderstorms always made people more sensitive. Sinus headaches, rheumatism... all sorts of things were aggravated by a falling barometer.

"This is it, Mr. Ridgeway," she said with relief, unclipping her harness as if she could hardly wait to escape.

Nor did she linger for him to open the door for her. Sliding out, she called her thanks over her shoulder. If he thought she was in an awful hurry, he could blame it on the rain. He could blame it on sunspots, for all she cared. All she knew was that she'd had about as much as she could take of Fate Ridgeway in close quarters. Next thing she knew, she would be wheezing again!

There were two chicken wings left, and a spoonful of potato salad. Sophie supposed she should feel flattered that someone liked her cooking. Thank goodness she hadn't invited Fate in for supper.

Not that they had that sort of relationship; not that she would want it. She finally had her life all comfortably arranged, and she was wise enough to know when she was well off. The last thing she needed was to get involved with another man. Especially another here-today, gone-tomorrow type.

If only she hadn't gotten herself trapped into going to that darned auction tomorrow night! It would be tough enough having to outbid every other woman there, without all the gossip and speculation it was bound to cause. *Poor old Sophie, who couldn't even hang on to someone like Phil Pennybaker, was bidding more than half her annual salary for a single date with her boss!*

Sophie blotted her forehead, a panicky look creeping into her normally calm gray eyes. "No big deal, Sophie," she whispered shakily. "All it takes is the hide of a rhinoceros, the nerve of a fire walker, and Fate's signature on a check. Piece of cake!"

With a groan, she stepped out of her clothes and began bracing herself for another sleepless night.

Three

As the day wore on, Fate found himself watching Sophie more and more, absorbing small things that might have escaped his notice if he hadn't just spent the better part of an evening wondering what was under that cool, emotionless exterior. Probably a cool, emotionless interior.

He knew she was dreading tonight; he was learning to read the small signs. Like hands that had developed a tendency to twist instead of resting quietly in her lap when she wasn't taking notes. Then there was that odd new trick she had of gasping every now and then, as if she'd forgotten to breathe until it was almost too late.

Hell, he'd been dreading the thing himself. He'd learned early in life, having gotten conned into attending too many hundred-dollar-a-plate dinners, that charity functions were pretty deadly affairs. The concerts weren't so bad, but a bachelor auction? In an unlikely place like Turbyville, South Carolina? Maybe he'd underestimated this town.

On the other hand, maybe he hadn't. There was something slightly barbaric about putting a man on the block and allowing women to haggle over him.

At least he'd fixed it so Sophie wouldn't have any competition in the bidding. A stack of books from the library, a few maps, a cheap plaid shirt and bow tie he'd picked up at the local variety store, and the glasses he wore when his eyes bothered him after too much close work—hardly the playboy image.

Actually, the trip he'd described was nothing more than an abbreviated version of the sort of holiday he'd always wanted to take. He wouldn't mind spending a few days wandering around the site of the oldest European settlement in the United States, examining fortifications and weaponry. Some of those cannons might actually have been duplicated in his father's foundry.

Fate shook off a tinge of guilt. There was nothing dishonorable or underhanded in what he'd done—or what he was planning to do. Just because he chose not to get all slickered up and hand out a line of bull about his "interests" and his "preferences in a date," that didn't mean he wasn't playing fair.

The truth was, his interest really *was* history, particularly the fifteenth to the seventeenth century. As for his preferences in dates—female, attractive, intelligent, and reasonably mature about covered it. No point in trying to describe that intangible quality that made one woman stand out among all the rest. Either it was there or it wasn't.

And either way, it had nothing to do with this business. He'd given his word, and he'd go through with it, but once the auction was over, that was it. He'd hand over the check and they could both get back to winding up preparations for Harry Chamus to take over the reins.

Fate spared a moment to think of Sophie's role. She'd dress for the occasion, of course—something quietly elegant. It would almost be worth checking it out just to see how she looked in something besides those starchy little cover-up jobs she wore to work.

Oh, he had no doubt she'd do it right—every inch The Serene Highness. At the appropriate moment, she'd lift her hand, give a regal nod, and that would be the end of it.

But just for a moment, suppose they were actually planning to go through with it, Fate mused. Going off somewhere together for a private holiday for two. And just suppose...

Fate jerked his thoughts back to reality. Suppose he got on with analyzing the figures he'd got from the cost department instead of wasting his time on a damned fairy tale!

Half an hour later he found himself staring off into space again, picturing Sophie's reaction when she saw his video. Maybe he shouldn't have spread it on quite so thick. The idea had been to discourage competition, but he hadn't thought about how she might feel, having to bid on the bumbling stuffed shirt he'd made himself out to be.

But what the devil—hadn't she been the one who'd steered him into the trap in the first place? Would he even have considered getting involved in any such tom-fool business if she hadn't practically forced him? Hadn't he offered to write a check and be done with it? If Ms. Pennybaker found herself in the hot seat, she had only herself to blame.

All the same, a woman like Sophie...

Fate never did finish that particular thought. But then, that was getting to be a habit lately, too. Thinking about Sophie. He'd find himself wondering about her at odd moments during the day—and the night— wondering the most irrelevant things. Such as what she wore to bed. If she slept on her back, or curled up on her side, or maybe on her stomach. Or what she did with her free time.

When he stopped to consider all the time he'd spent thinking about Sophie these past few weeks, it shook him up. She wasn't the most beautiful woman he'd ever known, not by a long shot. She sure as hell wasn't the most sophisticated, and yet, there was something about her...

It was a simple matter of policy with Fate never to get involved with a woman who worked with him. Things were bound to get sticky when the relationship broke up, as it inevitably did, because he wasn't looking for anything permanent. He valued his freedom too highly. Besides, in a few weeks he'd be finishing up here and heading north again.

Maybe he could hang around another week or so after Harry took over and he and Sophie could...

Nah, forget it. Something told him playing with Sophie would be about as safe as playing with a live grenade. She probably wouldn't be interested, anyway.

* * *

At four, Sophie gave up trying to concentrate and shut down her computer. It had been at least three years since she'd asked to leave early. She'd had a valid excuse that time; FloBelle and her candles had set fire to the downstairs living room, and a neighbor had called the fire department and then called Sophie.

This time no one had set fire to anything, as far as she knew, but she was leaving all the same. Retrieving her purse and buttoning the jacket of her gray linen suit, Sophie rapped softly on the closed door between the two offices. Fate had been in there alone for more than an hour now. He'd asked her to hold his calls when he'd come in from the plant, which meant he was probably working up another of his private and personal reports for the new owners.

"Mr. Ridgeway, I—" She opened the door and then halted in confusion, staring at the rumpled figure struggling to rise from the imported leather sofa that had been Mr. Potter's pride and joy.

"Oh, hell, Sophie, I—"

"Mr. Ridgeway, I didn't mean to intrude," Sophie said hurriedly, backing out. She would've pulled the door shut behind her, but Fate, his voice still gritty with sleep, waved her inside.

"Sorry about that, Sophie. I haven't been sleeping well lately, and when the mood suddenly struck me, I thought I could steal a quick one."

For reasons she didn't even begin to comprehend, Sophie felt compelled to make excuses for him. "You work too hard, Mr. Ridgeway. Everyone knows you're here before anyone else in the office, and you stay long after we've all gone home."

"Ever try to get anything done with a battery of phones ringing constantly and half the plant trooping in and out of your office?" Fate unself-consciously sucked in his breath and raked a palm over his flat abdomen, tucking his shirt securely under the belt of his dark, trim fitting trousers.

"That does seem to ring a bell," Sophie agreed dryly, and he acknowledged her irony with a twist of a smile. "I just wanted to tell you I was leaving now," she explained.

"Not asking my permission?"

"No, sir, announcing my intentions."

"Fair enough."

After Sophie left, Fate sat back down and put on his shoes, feeling somewhat better for his forty-five minute nap. He knew better than to run any piece of equipment flat out for as long as he'd been driving himself. Something was bound to give sooner or later.

So she was announcing her intentions, huh? That was a first in his experience. The woman was a marvel of quiet efficiency. What she didn't know about the inner workings of KellyCo Dye and Finishing wasn't worth knowing. They both knew he'd have had a hard time getting along without her, but not once had she presumed on that fact. This was the first time he'd known her to put her own needs ahead of the company's.

Probably going home early to get ready for tonight's shindig, he thought with a touch of amusement, wondering who her date was. Or did women go with a date to an affair when they were planning to bid on another man? The protocol in such a situation escaped him, but it would almost be worth getting shagged out in black tie just to—

Knock it off, Ridgeway, you're asking for trouble!

She wouldn't wear anything revealing, but it would be feminine and attractive. He pictured her in a soft shade of gray to match her eyes, something silky that skimmed her figure without being blatant about it. Her hair would be up, of course; she always wore it up. It would smell like whatever the stuff she washed it in—or maybe just for the occasion, perfume.

Would she wear perfume? Fate paused in the act of tying his right shoe and stared absently at the door to the outer office. His nostrils flared as he tried to imagine the scent she'd choose. Something light and feminine, like spring flowers. But subtle. The sort of perfume that didn't hit you all at once, but crept up on you gradually, with a hint of this, a nuance of that. Something complex...like Sophie.

He inhaled deeply, closing his eyes. Where would she put it? The backs of her knees? Her throat? Between her breasts? He could picture a pale, pink-tipped finger trailing a scented pathway down a milk-white valley between—

He swore softly. Leaping to his feet, he began to pace, pausing to adjust the fit of his trousers. Dammit, this was getting out of hand. The woman was his secretary, for heavens' sake! She was no more interested in him than he was in her—otherwise she wouldn't come to work every day smelling of nothing more seductive than soap, shampoo and toothpaste.

By nine-thirty, Sophie had bolted two Rolaids and three glasses of the club's champagne. She felt worse than ever. Finding a table near the back had been no problem, as everyone else seemed to want to be as close as possible to the large screen, on which the videotaped bachelors hawked their various wares.

Over on the far left of the room, a small dance band struggled to vent their music through a thicket of ferns and areca palms. The noise level had already risen to boiler-room proportions by the time she'd arrived, and the bidding hadn't even got under way.

Sophie had come alone. FloBelle and her friends had gone to have something or other read by a visiting psychic, and everyone else she'd asked already had a date.

No problem. She was probably better off alone. She'd had her ticket, her own transportation, and she'd known the way to the club. What more could she have needed? Now she was free to slip out as soon as she'd done what she had to do, with no one to complain about missing all the fun. Her gray chiffon dinner gown was years old, but it was still serviceable. The mothball smell was completely gone after a couple of days hanging out on the porch, and it still fit like a glove.

Now if she could only forget about her stomach long enough to see this thing through. She'd had a glass of champagne when she'd first arrived to give her something to do with her hands. And then she'd had another, because she'd been so tense. The Rolaids had come in there somewhere between the first and the second drink, because she really wasn't much of a drinker, but after seeing Fate's video, she'd snared a waiter and asked for a third.

The waiter, who used to bag groceries at the supermarket where Sophie shopped before he moved up in the world, had brought her a tray of munchies, for which she was profoundly grateful. It gave her something else to do with her hands, although raw cauliflower and chips weren't all that soothing to a rebellious digestive system.

With studied effort, she focused her attention on the screen, where a larger-than-life image of the assistant bank manager who'd asked her out several times after Phil had left, was describing what he planned to do for some lucky woman.

Sophie waited impatiently for Fate's video to come on again. The first time she'd seen it, she couldn't believe her eyes. The second time around, she'd wanted to strangle the man. By now, she wasn't sure if she was furious with him for making a joke of the whole thing, or amused because he'd had the nerve to do it.

One thing was certain: if he'd hoped to limit the amount of interest in his date package with that business about museums, libraries, and walking tours of some historical district, he was way off base. Judging from the comments she'd heard so far, he'd probably bring in the top bid of the evening.

"Sophie? What are you doing here all by yourself? Come join us, we have a table right up front."

Sophie looked up to see the woman she'd replaced as Clyde Potter's secretary five years before. She'd always liked Edna, who had taken early retirement when her husband had had a heart attack.

"Thanks, Edna, but I'm not staying long. I just wanted to see how the bidding went." Dear heavens, the man had her lying for him now!

"That's right, Dunwoody's your old alma mater, isn't it? I must say, I never realized until I took that tour with the Women's Service League last fall how run-down the old place was. From a distance, it looks like something out of *Gone With The Wind*."

"Before, or after Sherman?" Sophie inquired dryly, and the older woman laughed.

"Your new boss must be a joy to work for. What a marvelous sense of humor! Imagine, deliberately dolling himself up in that silly shirt and tie and talking about all that ancient history stuff. Although to tell the truth, after all those toothpaste smiles and preppy propositions, a leisurely tour of a museum and a few old forts sounds delightful. I wonder if Edgar would let me go."

Sophie managed to say something appropriate. Her head was beginning to spin just a bit. She was either going to have to beg a ride home or call a cab. "Edna, I wonder if I could get a ride home with you and Edgar? My head's beginning to ache, and I really don't feel like driving."

"Sure, honey, just say the word when you're ready to go. Edgar was ready five minutes after we got here, but since I'm on the committee, I thought I ought to stick around to see how things go."

"I'm with Edgar," Sophie muttered, blotting her forehead. Edna wandered off, and she waited for the ordeal to get under way. The sooner it began, the sooner she could go home. Right now, she'd have given her whole life savings to walk out of here and forget the whole thing, Dunwoody, Ridgeway and all.

Someone rapped on a microphone for attention, and gradually, the deafening noise died down to a modest roar.

"Ladies and gentlemen!" an amplified voice boomed across the noisy room. After a brief, but flowery tribute to the worthiness of the cause, the auctioneer moved directly to the business at hand. "You've seen them all, twelve good men, twelve brave souls who are willing to sacrifice themselves on the altar of sweet charity! Now, I know you're all anxious to wade in here and take your pick of the merchandise, ladies, but let's remember our manners. Any gentlemen who'd like to leave before it's too late may now do so."

Sophie swallowed hard and wiped her palms on her skirt as the audio system went through a short selection of screams and whistles. "All right now, ladies, what am I offered for a weekend cruise to the Bahamas aboard the—uh, that's the *Sea Devil*, folks! Fifty-eight feet, and she sounds like a real beauty. All the comforts of home! Bring your bikini, the gentleman says— if you really want to get formal! I have fifty, fifty, fifty, do I hear—"

The bidding quickly rose to five hundred twenty-five dollars, jumped to six hundred and stalled. The gavel sounded and there was a barrage of flashbulbs and champagne corks before the next bachelor was presented.

Later, Sophie couldn't recall much that had happened after that point. All she knew for certain was that she'd done it. She'd given her word she would, and she'd gone through with it. Fate was the third bachelor to go on the block. Considering the glamorous packages offered by the other eleven men, she hadn't known what to expect.

But then, considering the caliber of all men involved, she should have been prepared.

The girls from the office had started it. They'd been sitting as close to the front as possible. After that, one of the town's wealthiest widows had called out a bid of two hundred dollars, and that had started the avalanche. Before Sophie could even catch her breath, every available woman in town was shouting bids. One of them even offered her late husband's seventy-nine Cadillac that had been in the garage for five years.

"Face it, Sophie, these women know a solid hunk when they see one, even a hunk in a plaid shirt and a bow tie." Cleo Smithers from payroll had paused at Sophie's table, which happened to be on a direct route to the ladies' room. Cleo had dropped out after Mrs. Everly's two-hundred-dollar bid. "Too rich for my blood. I'll just stick to Saturday night at the steak house with Charlie, and a little hanky-panky for dessert. Aren't you going to make an offer? The girls down in payroll bet the ones from customer relations you'd walk off with the prize tonight. You've held out all these years for something special—well there he is. Go get 'im, honey!"

"Actually, I think I'm about ready to go home," Sophie said, enunciating carefully. "I had no idea it would be so noisy, did you? Why hire a band if you're not going to shut up long enough to listen to what they're doing?"

"Beats me, honey. Well, if you're leaving, I think I'll just wander back to the table and see if I can hedge a few bets." Both women gazed at the larger-than-life version of Fate's dark good looks as the auctioneer exhorted the audience to open their purses.

"Eight hunnert, eight, who'll gimme nine hunnert, nine, who'll gimme nine hunnert, nine, make it eight-fifty, folks, eight-fifty, who'll gi—"

"One thousand!" Sophie yelled out, leaping to her feet and waving her hands in the air.

A pall fell over the room. Cleo turned around and stared at her, eyes round and mouth hanging open. The drummer gave an unfinished drum roll, one of the horns made a squawk that sounded vaguely like a startled cow, and then the noise resumed as the next bachelor went on the block.

Somehow Sophie managed to survive the next few minutes. Half the plant seemed to be present, and most of them rushed to congratulate her. Her bid was duly recorded, and she signed a typed form that someone shoved in front of her. It could have been anything; she was beyond knowing or caring.

"—Her Serene Highness, would you believe it?" someone whispered loudly, and Sophie fought the urge to crawl under the table.

"Still waters run deep," another voice said knowingly.

"After being married to little Phily Pennybaker, anything in pants would look good. And that one looks great, even in a bow tie and glasses. I just hope she doesn't waste *all* her time in libraries and museums."

"You know Sophie—" someone else chimed in, and Sophie managed to duck through the crowd and find a place by the door. After tonight, not even *Sophie* knew Sophie!

Eventually she was rescued by Edna and Edgar, but not until she was back home in her own bedroom did it occur to Sophie that she'd spent only a fraction of what she'd been authorized to spend. There was no way in the world she could have jumped the bid to such a ridiculous sum. Maybe in Atlanta or New York or San Francisco a ten-thousand-dollar bid at a charity auction would have gone unnoticed. Here in Turbyville, it would've gone down in history.

Which meant that Dunwoody Home was out nine thousand dollars, thanks to her. Oh, Lord, what a mess! She'd ruined the fund drive, her stomach, and probably her reputation, too. It had been a lousy idea to start with—a bachelor auction! Why couldn't they have stuck to selling fruitcakes?

After a miserable night, Sophie woke with a headache and an assortment of vague misgivings. Confronting her pale image in the bathroom mirror, she tried to convince it that anyone who'd downed as many glasses of champagne as she had deserved to feel rotten.

She'd like to think that anyone who'd drunk all that champagne had probably imagined the whole mortifying episode, as well. It couldn't possibly have been as bad as she remembered—her friends betting on whether or not she'd bid on Fate, the remarks she'd overheard—her jumping up and screaming like a banshee in a whole roomful of people.

Everybody knew she didn't have that kind of money. They must really think she was desperate!

After a quick shower, Sophie felt marginally human. She put on a pair of thin sweatpants that dated from her last self-improvement period and a favorite yellow T-shirt. With a towel over her wet hair, she hurried down to the kitchen to make herself a pot of coffee.

FloBelle, barefooted and dressed in an old purple satin negligee, was already out in the front yard tend-ing her overcrowded flower beds. There was half a pot of cold herbal tea on the table, along with a dilapidated book that seemed to be shedding its pages.

While waiting for the coffee to brew, Sophie glanced at the book. *Gay's Illustrated Circle of Knowledge.* She could do with a dose of ancient wisdom about now.

Opening it at random, her eyes lit on a heading and she blinked and tried again. "Sex Life in the Vegetable World"? Oh, come on, now, she hadn't had all *that* much to drink last night! Three glasses of the stuff was hardly enough to hallucinate on twelve hours later!

The coffee gurgled, and so did Sophie's stomach. "—the stamen grows moist, and is perceptibly odorous," she read as she reached for her favorite mug. "Often it becomes greatly congested with..." *Oh, dear!*

She continued to skim the page as she poured coffee, added milk and sugar, and made her way slowly back upstairs. "—the powers of contraction... This condition is assumed not only by—" *Mmmm.* Without taking her eyes from the page, Sophie dragged the pad off her lounger and placed it on the deck. That way she could prop her head on the doorsill and see all eleven of her bird feeders.

Ignoring the busy feeders, she found her place on the yellowed old page and continued to read. "—but under other means of stimulation, as well. There is in some flowers a perceptible increase in heat. In those species where the stamen is longer than the pistil, the latter is observed to bend over and thus come into contact with the stamen at the right time."

Oh, dear, this was getting serious.

She was completely engrossed in the fecundation of plants, oblivious to the traffic jams around her feeders and the muted harmony of her fourteen wind chimes, when Fate Ridgeway appeared in the doorway over her head, looking pale and more than a little shaken.

Four

Fate had been feeling pretty rocky to start with. By the time he'd been taken by the hand and led through a waterfall of multicolored beads by an elderly cherub with long gray hair and mud-stained purple robes, he was ready to turn tail and run.

"I'm looking for Sophie Pennybaker," he'd said with a wary glance around him. "Is she here?"

The cherub had smiled benignly and patted his arm, her plump, beringed hand caked with grime. "Right up those stairs, honey. Go on up, she'll never hear you with all that ruckus in the backyard. When did you say you were born?"

With the stairway before him and the grubby, gray-haired cherub behind him, Fate hadn't hesitated. He'd taken the stairs two at a time, not daring to look back.

When was he born? What did that have to do with anything?

Reaching the top of the stairway, he'd stood in the light cast by a stained glass window and stared at the three closed doors.

"She's probably out on the porch," the purple cherub had called up after him. "Go on through the living room, the door on your left. She'll never hear you. Scorpio, aren't you? With some Capricorn and a little dab of Taurus? No wonder poor Sophie's been looking so ragged lately." As an afterthought she'd muttered something about "—some fire in there somewhere."

Fate had practically hurled himself through the door. Accustomed to working with all sorts of people, he'd never been particularly put off by strangers. But some strangers were stranger than others.

Finding himself in a large, sparsely furnished room, he'd taken stock, more curious than he cared to admit to see where Sophie lived. It was airy and light, with a minimum of comfortable looking furniture and a few attractive watercolors on the wall.

But no Sophie. "Pennybaker! Where the devil are you?" he called out. Spotting an open door half hidden by an angle of the wall, he strode forward, and then threw out his hands, catching himself on the doorframe just in time to keep from stepping on her.

"Mr. Ridgeway?" Sophie sat up quickly, nearly upsetting a half-filled coffee mug as a thick book slid off her lap.

"Sophie? Why didn't you call me last night? Didn't it occur to you that I might be—? What the devil is all that noise? Where did all those birds come from?"

The backyard, randomly wooded with tall pines, was alive with sound, color and motion. There were wind chimes and bird feeders of every description, plus a line of laundry and a couple of bright yellow metal chairs of a type he hadn't seen in twenty years. The railed porch was no more than twelve feet square, and Sophie had been sprawled out on a padded cushion on the floor, her head on the doorsill, with a perfectly good chaise lounge not three feet away.

His secretary! Her prim and proper Serene Highness.

Evidently she'd been drying her hair. A moment ago it had been spread out across a towel, and now it was tumbling around her shoulders like a skein of spun gold. Her feet were bare, her pink unvarnished toenails looking incredibly vulnerable, and it was pretty obvious from the way the T-shirt she was wearing followed the contours of her body, that she wasn't exactly over-burdened with underwear, either.

Fate swallowed hard. He couldn't think of a thing to say. At the moment, he couldn't even remember why he was there.

"Mr. Ridgeway?" Sophie murmured, closing the book and then hastily adjusting several loose pages.

And then he remembered. After his unscheduled afternoon nap, he'd had more trouble than ever falling asleep, and his restless mind had kept playing back that damned video he'd made for the auction. What had seemed like a great idea at first, insuring that she wouldn't have any competition and could make her bid and leave with as little fuss as possible, had suddenly struck him as wildly inappropriate.

With a stretch that bared a sliver of back, Sophie leaned forward and placed her mug on a low table. After that first startled moment, her face had grown completely still, her thoughts, as usual, a complete mystery to him. But there was no way she could hide the glorious fall of hair she'd been keeping screwed to the back of her head all these months.

There ought to be a law against hiding something that lovely, Fate thought resentfully. Sunlight glistened on the tips of her lashes and bathed her skin with a radiance that made it look almost translucent.

Or was there some other reason for that translucent look? Come to think of it, there were distinct shadows under her eyes that hadn't been there when she'd left the office yesterday.

"Won't you have a seat, Mr. Ridgeway," she invited stiffly.

Fate sat. Or rather he braced his hips on the railing, hooking his heel on the lower rail and crossing his arms over his chest. He should've waited until Monday. Evidently he needed a more structured setting to keep his mind under control. This was going to be tough enough without his going off on a tangent and getting all stirred up.

"Uh, Sophie—about last night..." He cleared his throat, stroked his chin a few times and then rammed one hand in the pocket of his pants. How the hell did he apologize for pulling a damfool stunt, and then, in the very next breath, tell her that unless one of them could come up with a valid excuse, they were going to have to go through with the whole works?

"Yes, Mr. Ridgeway?" Back ramrod straight, Sophie curled her legs around beside her, folded her hands on her lap and waited. She was furious. He'd come to gloat! The least he could've done was to wait until Monday.

"How'd it go?" he asked, his voice grating over her raw nerves.

"The auction, you mean?" Of course he meant the auction! What else would he mean? "I got you for a thousand dollars. I told you I was no good at these things."

Fate's jaw dropped. "What's that old line they use in bad movies? I may be cheap, but I'm not easy."

"I'm sorry if that hurts your pride, Mr. Ridgeway. Believe me, I wanted Dunwoody to have all that money, but things just aren't that expensive around here, not even men."

"Don't worry about it, Sophie, I'll make out the check for the full amount I promised," he dismissed easily. "Look, have you had any calls lately?"

"Calls? You mean phone calls?"

He tugged at the open collar of his soft knit shirt as if it were strangling him. "Right. More specifically, calls from a reporter from the local scandal sheet."

Sophie felt a growing wariness. The *Turbyville Times* answered to that description, all right. Most of the townspeople subscribed to the Columbia paper, but *all* of them read the *T'ville Times*, which was two-thirds ads and one-third gossip. No one dared miss an issue for fear of seeing their name in print. Petra George covered everything from the fistfight that had broken out at the last school-board meeting to who was seen with whom at five in the morning in the back seat of a late model Cadillac at Buster's Used Cars.

"I unplugged my phone last night," she admitted. "I guess I forgot to plug it in again." After the third call from a coworker wanting to know when she was planning to run off to Florida with her purchase, she'd had no choice.

"That explains why I couldn't get you on the phone. I wanted to warn you about that reporter. I forget her name, but she's the same one who tackled me in the parking lot the other day—leggy brunette about twenty-five or so, big red-rimmed glasses and the finesse of a drill sergeant. Seems she's covering the whole Dunwoody business, starting with the auction. She's not only planning to see each couple off, she'll be at the airport to greet 'em when they get back." A timely gust of warm wind set off the chimes again, drowning out his next few words, which was just as well.

Sophie propped her elbows on her up-drawn knees and her chin on her fists. "Oh, that's just great! Since Petra George took over for her uncle, no one's been safe around here. Her father was a famous war correspondent, and she worships the ground he walked on, but darn it, this is no war zone! Why can't she just—" She sighed. "Well, at least we don't have anything to worry about."

"I beg your pardon?" Fate had missed half of what she was saying. How the devil was he supposed to concentrate when every time she leaned forward, there was a gap of several inches between the elastic waist of her trousers and the knit band of her shirt. From the effect it was having on him, you'd think he was allergic to skin.

Sophie sighed and lifted her head, thus covering all but a tiny sliver of pale skin. "I said at least it doesn't concern us. We're not going anywhere, remember? We've done our bit for dear old Dunwoody, and now we can get back to work. Oh, by the way, did I tell you I have a lead on a house for your Mr. Chamus?"

"Sophie, you're not listening, dammit. What are we going to do about that woman? Put out a contract on her? Keep on postponing the date until she forgets and goes on to something else?"

"Petra forgets like an elephant forgets," Sophie said dryly. "I've known her ever since she came to town. Believe me, I know."

"Okay, so we jump the gun and take off right away without telling her."

"Take off on what? For where? I thought this was supposed to be a date in name only."

"Would you like to have your dragon journalist on our backs from now on?"

"But it's not fair! We did our part—the only part that matters, anyway."

"Don't tell me, tell your friend the ferret. I'm the one who wanted to mail in a check and be done with it, remember? In fact, this whole mess is all your fault, Sophie."

"*My* fault!"

"You heard me. But the question now is what are we going to do about it?"

"All right, I'm thinking, I'm thinking!" Sophie gestured irritably for silence, totally unaware of how out of character she was acting.

Fate watched her frown of concentration, his scowl easing as frustration gradually gave way to fascination. "As I see it, we've got no choice but to go through with it," he reasoned. "That's the simplest solution in the long run."

"Oh, sure, it's all so simple," Sophie scoffed. "Just when do you propose we take off? You have three meetings next week you can't afford to miss, Mr. Chamus is supposed to fly down to look at houses and go over the preliminaries with you, and I've got all those—"

"There's the weekend," Fate suggested.

"Fine. You're meeting the ATW people Saturday morning, but we could take off Saturday afternoon and come back Sunday morning."

"Oh, hell!" Launching himself away from the railing, Fate began to pace the confined space, stepping over the flowered plastic pad, the battered book with the faded gold lettering, and Sophie's feet. "That would give rise to even more speculation, I suppose. They'll wonder what you did that scared me into cutting things short," he said with a wry attempt at humor.

Sophie sent him a scathing look from under a tangle of drying hair. He couldn't know how close to the mark he was—or could he? "I'm beginning to think we made a mistake by getting involved in the first place. Anywhere else you could just sweep it under the rug and forget it, but in Turbyville that's the first place people think to look."

From a distance of five feet he turned and scowled at her. "Then what do you suggest, Mrs. Pennybaker? That we give them something to talk about? Shall I throw you over my saddle and ride off into the sunset?"

Sophie was still feeling the results of three glasses of champagne and all those antacid tablets, not to mention the raw cauliflower. Her head ached, her stomach was in a state of rebellion, and she was in no mood to take the blame for anything. "What do you mean, what do *I* suggest? The truth is, Mr. Ridgeway, this was as much your fault as it was mine. You agreed to it, didn't you?"

Two quick strides and he was standing over her, one of his moccasins practically shoved up against her bare toes. "You just won't do the decent thing and accept the blame, will you, Pennybaker? And here I thought you were such a great secretary."

"What?" Sophie glared at him. "I'm the best secretary you've ever had, and you damned well know it!"

"Who the devil railroaded me into attending that meeting at the barbecue place? Who was it who insisted that it was in the best interests of the company to get involved in community affairs?"

"All right, I admit I might just possibly have influenced you to some small degree, but—"

"Oh, come on now, don't be so modest," Fate taunted. And then he sighed and raked a hand through his hair. "Look, Sophie, this isn't solving our problem. As I see it, we have only one course of action." He waited for some sign that she was at least willing to listen, but she remained stubbornly silent. Where was his old secretary, the quiet, efficient woman who'd anticipated his needs before he'd even been aware of them himself?

Clearing his throat, Fate leaned back against the railing. He could have done with a cup of coffee, but he knew better than to ask. There was something about his relationship with Sophie that was different lately. He couldn't put his finger on it, but he'd been around enough artillery to recognize a potentially explosive situation when one confronted him.

"Where was I? Oh, yeah—one course of action. Okay, so we set aside a block of time when there's nothing particularly pressing, and we drive up to Columbia and catch a plane to Saint Augustine. If this George woman wants to see us off, it'll all look on the up-and-up. We'll have nothing to hide."

"Of course we'd have nothing to hide, we'd be giving in. Knuckling under. I thought the whole idea was to go through the motions without actually committing to anything."

"You said yourself that might not be ethical," Fate reasoned.

"That was the bid-rigging part. Where you put in the fix and I got you."

"So what's the difference, once we're off the ground, we can forget the auction and go our separate ways. All we have to do is show up together on the return trip."

"I don't know," she said cautiously. "It all sounds pretty sneaky to me. I've never been any good at intrigue. I can't even play a decent game of bridge."

Fate ran his hand impatiently through his hair, leaving it standing on end. "Dammit, there's nothing sneaky about it. Look, I've worked the devil out of you for nearly four months now, and I haven't spared myself, either. We've put in some tough time, and I could do with a break before we tackle the last phase. I know damned well you could, too, if you weren't too stubborn to admit it. If we can put an end to this Dunwoody thing and at the same time, spend a relaxing weekend, where's the harm?"

Sophie began tapping her bare toes soundlessly on the cushion, a habit she had when she was thinking. "I've never been to Florida. Is it nice?"

Fate nodded. "The parts I've seen. Saint Augustine'll be new to me, too, though."

She couldn't know how wistful she looked, Fate thought, narrowing his eyes as he studied the woman who was still curled up like a kid on a faded cushion on the floor. South Carolina and Florida were practically next-door neighbors. Where had she been all her life? He'd thought every kid spent at least one Easter vacation at Fort Lauderdale. He had, hoping to find a fort. He'd been happy to settle for exploring for girls, instead.

"Actually, my father was something of a history buff," he said, making it sound as if he were confessing something vaguely shameful.

It was the first time to Sophie's knowledge that he'd ever volunteered a shred of personal information of any kind since he'd come south. He might be rather nice once she got to know him.

Not that she would, of course. They'd go their separate ways, he'd said, and that was just fine with her.

"It's settled, then? You'll go?"

"It's been years since I went anywhere exciting. It might be rather nice."

"I'm afraid it's the wrong season," Fate said, seemingly more relaxed now that it had been decided. "Winter would be better, but by next winter, I'll be up in Maine, reorganizing another plant."

Sophie uncoiled and rose to her feet. "Well... I suppose if we're really going, I'd better get busy. I have a thousand things to do."

Fate cleared his throat again and managed to tear his bemused gaze away from the sight of his prim and proper secretary, barefooted, her hair a silky snarl around her face, and a few dozen freckles in plain view. Either they'd just now popped out, or he'd been remiss in not noticing them before. "Yeah. Well...I guess I'd better shove off. Glad that's all settled, anyway. See you Monday, huh?"

"Monday," Sophie murmured, puzzled by a return of the restlessness that had afflicted her so much lately. Too much champagne, that was all it was, she told herself. It had nothing at all to do with seeing Fate on her own back porch, wearing chinos that were soft and body conforming, with a cotton knit pullover that clung faithfully to every muscle on his chest. She'd known all along that he was tall and well built, but somehow, seen in these circumstances, he exuded a raw sensuality that abraded her already ragged nerves.

That damned book she'd been reading! Sexy vegetables indeed!

"Well. Okay, I guess I'll be running along, then." Fate stepped over the cushion and up into the living room, and Sophie was drawn along behind him like a scrap of paper caught in a back draft. Just as he reached the opposite door, he turned back. "Sophie, there was this woman out in your yard..."

"FloBelle," Sophie said quickly with her first real smile of the day. She could well imagine what he must have thought, meeting her mother-in-law for the first time. Flo didn't stand on ceremony. "She's my ex-husband's mother. We share the house."

* * *

When Monday came, both Fate and Sophie were too busy even to think about the upcoming trip. Petra George stopped by Sophie's office shortly before she left for the day, wanting to know exactly when they planned to take off.

"As soon as we can find time," Sophie said rather tartly. Over the weekend, she'd actually begun to get into the spirit of things, window-shopping for beach clothes and chunky summer jewelry. All it took was a single question from Pet to remind her that this was essentially a business trip. It might be for a good cause, but somehow, remembering all the junkets taken by former CEOs, their families and friends, the yacht cruises and flights in corporate jets to hunting clubs, horse races, golf matches and bowl games, it was a bit too much for her prickly conscience.

Sophie knew very well how much money had been wasted in the past by men who had done little or nothing to earn it. They'd taken KellyCo the way Sherman's army had taken Atlanta, leaving the ruins in the hands of tired old figureheads like Clyde Potter when they moved on to some other unlucky victim. Most of them had known little or nothing about textiles, and not one of them had owned more than a few token shares of stock. KellyCo's future as a going concern meant nothing to them as long as the company coffers could provide the salaries, enormous bonuses and perks they demanded.

Sophie tried to tell herself that as comptroller of Bannerman International, Fate would know whether or not they could afford such a grand gesture. And it was for charity, after all. It wasn't like the private hunting lodge or the yacht bought with company funds that had somehow wound up missing from the company's net assets after the last CEO had left for greener pastures.

It was Bannerman's money, she reminded herself, and Bannerman was calling the shots. All the same, ten thousand dollars for a couple of days in Florida? Somehow it made them sound every bit as bad as the greediest of the transient CEOs who'd picked Kelly-Co's bones clean and moved on in search of fatter prey.

"What's wrong, Sophie?"

Sophie glanced up sharply. She'd completely forgotten Pet was still here, which only went to show how this thing was getting to her. "Nothing, Pet, just too much to do and too little time, as usual. Was that all you wanted?"

"Hardly," the brunette said with an engaging grin, "but I'll leave you to it. Let me know as soon as you set the date, will you? Cooperate with me and I promise I'll try not to be too obnoxious."

Sophie waited a few minutes to compose herself and then rapped on Fate's door. "Could I see you for a minute, Mr. Ridgeway?"

Fate nodded to the chair, and Sophie seated herself on the edge, knees together, feet together, hands folded in her lap. "If this is out of line, I'm sorry, but—are you sure KellyCo can afford you? I mean, we were in pretty bad shape when Bannerman came along, and I'm not sure we ought to be throwing around that kind of money, even for a good cause."

Fate's eyes widened. "You're asking if I'm worth the money they're paying me? What do you want me to do, let you put me through one of my own five-minute tests?"

"I'm not talking about your salary, I'm talking about throwing away ten thousand dollars for a weekend in Florida."

"You're afraid I won't be worth it?" His lips twitched as if he were having trouble concealing a smile. "Sophie, I promise you, you'll get your money's worth—the full amount, even if you did get me at a cut-rate price."

She promised herself she would not blush. She wouldn't lose her temper. The man was baiting her and, as her boss, she supposed he had that privilege. Up to a point, after which she'd take the top of his head off if he even looked at her crooked. There was a limit to her good nature. "My apologies, Mr. Ridgeway, I was completely out of line. You're certainly in a position to know whether or not KellyCo can afford such a grand gesture."

Fate's chair tipped forward and his arms came down on the desk. "Sophie, this is none of your business, but since it seems to worry you so much, I'll tell you anyway. The check will be written against my personal account. KellyCo will get the public credit and I'll get the tax write-off, and now, if that's all, I suggest you see if you can get through to Crane at EPA and set up a meeting at the Cow Creek plant next week. We may as well get that drainage business settled once and for all."

Sophie felt like crawling out of his office. Backward. With a few obeisances along the way. She should have realized he was different from all the other fly-by-night boy wonders. She *had* realized it, only she still found it hard to open up and trust anyone. "I'm truly sorry, Mr. Ridgeway," she said, looking back from the door that separated the two offices.

This time he smiled. It was a genuine smile, with eyes and lips and that intriguing crease in his left cheek all coming into play. "Sophie, just for the record, how did I do compared to the other bachelors? After that stunt I pulled, I don't suppose I walked away with top honors," he said, looking remarkably like a small boy who was hoping that the fact that he'd swept up the mess would make up for the fact that he'd broken the cookie jar.

Sophie melted. Was there a man anywhere who didn't possess a tender ego? "Hardly," she said gently. "However, you didn't win the booby prize, either. That went to Handy Withers. His real name's Horace, but he earned the nickname, at least among the women, by—uh..."

"I can imagine," Fate finished, grinning broadly. And then the grin faded, to be replaced by the more familiar scowl. "Okay, so let me know when you can schedule our so-called date, and we'll get it out of the way."

Their so-called date was postponed twice because of business emergencies, and in desperation, they set it for Memorial Day weekend, giving them Monday as a travel day. Fate grudgingly conceded that as long as they had to go, they might as well stay the requisite length of time, and Sophie gleefully ordered the tickets from the town's only travel agent.

She had trouble getting reservations, but the agent thought she might be able to wangle a couple of seats on a flight that left late Friday afternoon. "We'll take it," Sophie replied quickly. "Now, what about hotels? Do you know anything about the ones in Saint Augustine?"

By the time she was assured of two tickets to Jacksonville, a rental car to drive them to Saint Augustine and three nights at a hotel that was perfectly situated for both their tastes, she was as excited about the trip as if she'd actually planned the whole thing.

Dutifully, she called the *Turbyville Times* and left word of their departure date for Petra George. She'd promised, after all, and Sophie never went back on a promise, but after all this time, surely the bachelor auction was stale news.

No such luck.

"All right now, Sophie, put your arm around his waist and wave—no, get closer! And smile!" The whip-slender brunette bent her knees to get the angle she wanted. Pet was her own photographer, as the newspaper's budget didn't allow a professional. "Okay, that's great! See you two when you get back."

Sophie dropped her arm instantly. Fate was a little slower in dropping his. "We'll have to remember to get a tan," he said under his breath, "or she'll think we spent the whole time in bed."

Sophie caught her breath but recovered quickly. "Don't worry, I plan to spend my whole holiday on the beach. Maybe you can find a museum with a skylight," she quipped, and then smiled when it occurred to her that she was actually teasing the man. That was a first.

"Just full of the holiday spirit, aren't we?"

Sophie bit her lip, but her eyes were dancing. Fate laughed down at her softly, but no sooner were they settled in their seats than he opened his briefcase and took out a stack of reports. Sophie was too excited to care. This whole thing was a brand-new adventure for her, and she didn't intend to miss a single moment of it. She fastened her seat belt, listened carefully to the stewardess's recitation, and then explored the contents of the pocket on the back of the seat in front of her.

And then they were rolling. She gripped the armrests and stared out the small patch of Plexiglas as the landscape began to blur. She never even felt them leave the ground, but suddenly her stomach lurched. Her whole perspective had changed! She was looking down on things she'd never before looked down on.

Fate rustled impatiently through the papers in his lap, but Sophie didn't even notice. There were cars down there, looking like Matchbox toys. Several outdoor swimming pools became a scattering of aquamarines. Forehead pressed against the window, she was oblivious to the man beside her.

Suddenly there were two distinct thuds, as if something had exploded right below her seat. She'd heard them. She'd even felt them! A feeling of cold dread swept over her, followed almost immediately by a feeling of deep regret for all the things she'd left undone in this life.

They were going to crash!

Closing her eyes, Sophie pressed her head back against the seat and tried desperately to recall what the stewardess had said about emergency landings. Her breath was coming in shallow little gasps, and she felt moisture bead her upper lip as a stream of icy air from the overhead blower struck her face.

"Sophie, are you all right? You're not going to be sick, are you?" Fate's voice beat against the shell of terror that insulated her. "Sophie! Honey, what's the matter? If you need to get out, just say so. There's a bag in the—"

"Didn't you hear it?" she whispered fiercely.

"Hear what?" Fate shoved the papers heedlessly into his briefcase and pried one of her hands loose from the armrest. It was freezing cold. Every freckle on her face stood out in bold relief. "Why didn't you tell me you got airsick? I'd have called the whole thing off, reporter be damned."

Turning so that her lips were no more than an inch away from his ear, she said tensely, "Mr. Ridgeway, something exploded. Two somethings. I heard it distinctly, and I felt it, too."

Puzzled, Fate knew only that she was terrified, and Sophie didn't terrify without a cause. He made a quick scan of the interior of the plane, seeing nothing out of the ordinary. The stewardesses were trundling out the beverage cart, and he knew damned well they'd be strapped in if something was going sour.

On the other hand his unflappable Sophie was definitely coming unglued. Releasing his seat belt, he lifted the armrest between them so that he could draw her closer. She didn't need any encouragement. Like a rabbit one jump ahead of a fox, she burrowed into his side as if her very life were at stake.

"Sophie? Honey, tell me just what you thought you heard."

"I didn't think anything," she retorted, "I *heard* it. It wasn't loud, and it sounded as if it were right underneath where we're sitting. Two distinct thuds, one after the other. The pilot's not saying anything because he doesn't want us to panic, but we've got to do something!"

Understanding dawned suddenly, and Fate's arm tightened around her. God, she was trembling all over. His Sophie. His formidable little princess! Who would've thought she'd turn out to be so timid?

Five

"Honey, we're not going to crash," Fate assured her. "What you heard was only the wheels collapsing into their housing."

"Collapsing!" Sophie gasped softly. She caught only the single word, but it was enough to fuel her imagination. First the wheels went, then the wings, then the whole body would disintegrate. And for reasons she couldn't begin to fathom, the pilot seemed hell-bent on having it happen as far above ground as possible!

A new thought occurred to her, and she moaned and burrowed her head in the hollow of Fate's shoulder. The pilot was being held hostage by a madman. They were being hijacked, and the perpetrators were determined that there would be no witnesses. Oh, Lord, why hadn't she stayed on solid, South Carolina earth where she belonged?

Fate gently pried her fingers loose from his thigh, clasping both her small, icy hands in his. "Sophie, listen to me. We're not going to crash. Nothing exploded. Look around you, do you see anyone in a panic? Would the stewardess be rolling out the beverage cart if we were going down?"

Opening one eye, Sophie examined the shoulder of a man across the aisle, one seat forward. He was reading the sports page of the *Atlanta Constitution*. If they were going down, at least he'd know the score, she told herself, and with that irreverent thought, reason began to seep back into her paralyzed brain.

"You're certain we're all right?" she asked, not quite ready yet to give up the security of the arms that held her.

"We're fine. If the wheels had *not* retracted, then I'd have been worried, too. With that much drag we couldn't have gained any altitude, at least not without doubling our fuel consumption."

"Oh." With the one small comment, Sophie began to disengage herself, pretending for all she was worth that she hadn't just made a complete fool of herself.

Fate let her go with a smile that was more tender than he could have imagined. Watching her smooth her hair and brush at a crease in her skirt, he was conscious of a feeling of emptiness where her body had rested against his.

"Well!" she said brightly, assuming a composure she hadn't quite managed to achieve. "I'm sorry if I embarrassed you, Mr. Ridgeway. I—uh, I haven't done a whole lot of flying."

Fate overcame the temptation to take her back in his arms and offer her more comfort. Embarrassment didn't quite describe the way he'd felt. Satisfaction came closer to the mark, but still missed the target. He'd always scoffed at the machismo mystique, but maybe there was something to be said for this he-man stuff, after all.

A bit gruffly, he said, "I think we can dispense with formality, Sophie. Call me Fate—or L.L., if you prefer." Before she could respond, he went on. "How much flying have you done?"

"Actually, none," Sophie confessed. She watched the smile tug at the corner of his mouth, and she stiffened defensively. "It's hardly a crime. There has to be a first time for everything." Turning away, she pressed her face against the window and began to watch the patchwork panorama unfolding below. When cottony clouds eclipsed the view, she pulled out a copy of the airline's magazine and pretended an interest in an article on the six best golf courses in the South.

She could feel Fate's gaze on her, tightening her nerves until she could have screamed. "What's the matter," she burst out finally, cramming the magazine back into the seat pocket. "Haven't you ever seen a dodo bird before? There must be thousands of people who've never flown. Millions, probably."

"I'm sure you're right," Fate agreed equably.

His calmness only added to her irritation. "There might even be a few things *you* haven't done."

"Lots of them."

Still she couldn't let it drop, not when she was seething with unspent emotional energy that had to be discharged before it made her physically ill. "I've probably even done a few things you haven't," she claimed recklessly.

"No doubt." Fate was openly smiling by now.

"Such as..." Such as what? She couldn't come up with a single example, at least none that sounded very impressive. Of course, she'd once been married. But then, perhaps he had, too.

"I expect we both have a few discoveries left to look forward to, Sophie," Fate said gently. For the first time in the nearly four months he'd known her, it occurred to him to wonder what her husband had been like— what they'd been like together. And why, for a thirty-three-year-old woman who'd been married and divorced, she still seemed so remarkably unawakened.

Which led directly to another thought, one which Fate shoved firmly from his mind. Until the reorganization at KellyCo was finished, he didn't have time to get involved with any woman. And even if he had, he'd hardly have chosen someone like Sophie Pennybaker. They hadn't a thing in common outside working hours. He was a loner by nature and a bachelor by choice whose experience with the opposite sex was extensive, if selective.

Sophie, on the other hand, was a timid soul under that brisk facade, who seemed perfectly content to drift along forever in a dead-end job, watching birds and looking after that dotty mother-in-law of hers. As for experience...

It was there that his imagination hit a snag every time. Fate had never had any trouble recognizing signals from a woman, whether he returned her interest or not. But if Sophie had given him so much as a single thought in that respect, he'd sure as hell missed it. All of which made this whole line of thought utterly meaningless! Hauling his briefcase out from under the seat, he took out a handful of papers and made a pretense of concentrating.

The clouds thinned, and once again Sophie turned her attention to the Georgia woodland below. Or rather, she turned her face. Her attention was not so easily directed, not when her body was still tingling as if lightning had struck nearby.

She made a deliberate effort to erase from her mind the feel of warm, hard muscles, the scent of clean linens, masculine toiletries, and something that was essentially male. He'd murmured words of reassurance, words she'd absorbed and promptly forgotten, but she couldn't forget the sound of his voice. For once it had lacked the usual edge of impatience.

And *she* lacked her usual edge of common sense, Sophie thought disgustedly. Just because she'd gotten a little upset—just because he'd held her and comforted her for a few minutes, that didn't mean their relationship had changed. Any stranger with a degree of humanity would have done as much, and it would have meant as little.

So she'd overreacted. Under the circumstances it had been perfectly understandable. The fact was that she'd been keyed up before she'd even boarded the flight, and then, before she'd had a chance to settle down, the darn wheels had bumped the belly of the plane and scared her out of her wits. And on top of that, Fate had grabbed her and held her.

Good gosh, who wouldn't overreact? At least she hadn't started wheezing. That would've been the final indignity. What was it her cottage mother used to say about her? "Sophie's overstimulated; she just wants attention."

Well, this time Sophie hadn't wanted attention, but there was no denying that she was overstimulated. *Boy*, was she overstimulated! The sooner they got to Saint Augustine and went their separate ways, the better she'd like it.

She pretended to doze throughout the remainder of the flight until a stewardess passed by, checking to be sure all seats were in an upright position and all seat trays and loose luggage secured for landing. Sophie silently congratulated herself on having passed inspection.

Opening her purse, she angled the mirror of her compact so that she could check her appearance. It was reassuringly familiar. Same gray eyes, same tan hair, same freckles that seemed to blossom each year about the time the azaleas were at their peak.

On impulse, she took out the tiny vial of perfume she'd impulsively splurged on the day she'd picked up the airline tickets. It was French, sinfully expensive, and the tiny drop she'd daubed on her wrist that morning had smelled heavenly, but it had long since worn off. Perhaps another drop would bolster her spirits for the landing.

She was struggling with the snug-fitting glass stopper when Fate reached for it. "Here, let me do that for you," he said impatiently.

"It's not important," Sophie said hastily. He'd probably think she was using it for his benefit, and that wasn't the case at all. "I can do it myself," she argued, yanking as he grabbed. The stopper that had resisted her best efforts suddenly gave way, dashing the fragrant contents of the vial across Fate's lap.

Stricken, Sophie could only stare at him. His eyes swiftly lost their pine green hue and took on the icy, winter-pond look as the scent of French lilacs eddied up from his thighs, borne on the heat from his body.

"I suppose you think it's funny," Fate snapped.

The sports fan from across the way craned his neck and sniffed, and Sophie struggled to overcome a sudden urge to giggle. "No I don't," she lied. She was only dimly aware of the fact that they had touched down and were now zooming toward the terminal. It was impossible to look away from Fate's face, and even as she watched, a tide of color spread over his angular features.

From somewhere behind them, a child's voice rose over the roar of the jet engines. "Mama, I smell something pretty; is it Flor'da yet?"

The mother hushed her child, and Sophie managed to tear her gaze away. She was going to have to apologize—and she would, too. Just as soon as she was certain she could open her mouth without breaking into gales of hysterical laughter.

The moment they came to a halt, passengers flooded the aisle. Fate and Sophie were trapped in their seats until the sluggish tide began to move. Meanwhile all around them, people were sniffing and eyeing them curiously. By the time they were able to leave the plane, Fate was rigid with embarrassment.

At least Sophie hoped it was embarrassment and not anger. It really wasn't her fault that he reeked of French lilacs. If he hadn't insisted on using brute force on her tiny perfume bottle, it never would have happened.

"Come on, let's collect our bags and get the hell out of here," he said gruffly, grabbing her by the wrist and practically dragging her along the concourse.

"Why don't you go on ahead," Sophie panted as she hurried to keep up with him. "Your legs are longer than mine."

He spared her a single withering look. "Where *I* go, *you* go. As long as I smell like a streetwalker's convention, I'm damned well going to have someone along to deflect the blame."

"Streetwalker!" Sophie squawked, and then quickly lowered her voice as heads turned their way. "That's genuine French perfume! Just that teensy tinsy bottle cost more than—"

"I don't care if that *teensy tinsy bottle*," he mimicked her tone of indignation, "was a personal gift from Marie Antoinette. Until I can get to a hotel and change into something that doesn't smell to high heaven, you're going to be glued to my side, lady! I've had all the funny looks I can take."

And glued she was. Nor did she find much comfort in Fate's embrace this time. Side by side, hip to hip, thigh brushing thigh, they strode through the airport, Fate's arm around her waist and his fingers biting into her flesh. By the time they reached the baggage area, Sophie, gasping for breath, had decided that she'd quite had her fill of the scent of lilacs, French or otherwise.

It was almost completely dark by the time they loaded the luggage into the trunk of the rental car. Sophie was wilting fast. She'd risen early, too excited to sleep, and since daybreak, she'd been going flat out, hardly stopping to eat. She was starved, but Fate showed no signs of wanting to stop for a meal.

But then, perhaps that wouldn't be such a good idea, after all. The waiter would probably take one whiff and invite them to leave.

"How about checking the city map and seeing if you can navigate us to our hotel," Fate suggested once they'd cleared the sprawling outskirts of Jacksonville and were headed south on I-95.

Sophie dug out the map they'd got from the rental desk and then rechecked the name and address of their hotel. "We're booked into a place called the Hotel de Aviles on Avenida Menendez. It's supposed to be close to both the museums and the beach, and according to the travel agent, we're lucky to've gotten anything on such short notice at this time of year. You take a left on State Road 16, a right on San Marco when we get into Saint Augustine, and that feeds into Avenida Menendez. The hotel will probably have a sign out front."

"Thanks, Sophie. Remind me always to travel with my secretary."

"Remind your secretary to leave her perfume at home next time," Sophie retorted, which was as close to an apology as she felt like offering.

"Let's just hope the night clerk's lost his sense of smell."

"I think you're beginning to air out," she said hopefully. "Or maybe I'm just starting to get used to you."

"You'd better hope so," Fate said darkly, but there was an undercurrent of laughter in his voice.

Sophie leaned back, closed her eyes and began to make plans. Dinner had first priority. Room service if possible, because she wasn't sure she had enough energy left to go out and hunt up a restaurant. Tomorrow, first thing, she'd head for the beach and get started on her vacation. She'd stocked up on sunscreen and brought along two paperback novels, one for each day of her vacation. She intended to make up for all the vacations she'd ever missed. It had been years since she'd gone anywhere alone—driving Flo to visit her Aunt Patty in Tuscaloosa last year hardly constituted a vacation.

She made a mental note to call home as soon as she got settled in. Flo had insisted she'd be fine by herself, but Sophie couldn't help but worry. Phil had written that he'd like to have his mother move to Hobbs, New Mexico, where he and his new family were running a small restaurant, but Flo didn't seem particularly interested in leaving the old house on River Street, and as long as she was there, Sophie felt responsible for her welfare.

"So what are your plans, Sophie?" Fate asked as he turned off onto San Marco Avenue.

"My what? Oh—my plans. To catch up on my rest. Catch up on my reading. Swim in the ocean until I'm waterlogged, and eat seafood at least twice a day. I'd spend twenty-four hours a day on the beach if I weren't afraid of being picked up for vagrancy. I've always loved the beach—at least, I think I have."

Fate shot her a speculative look. Somehow, the thought of Sophie in a bathing suit, salty, sandy, and windblown as she plunged into the surf, was rather disturbing. "What do you mean, you *think* you've always loved the beach?"

"Actually, I've only been twice. The first time was when I went to Myrtle Beach on my honeymoon. I ended up getting blistered so badly we had to leave early. FloBelle kept me wrapped up in poultices soaked in strong tea until I had to go back to work. I was so disappointed, I cried for days."

Fate chuckled, finding the thought of a tea-swaddled Sophie enchanting, tears or not. "Hardly the perfect honeymoon," he conceded. "Hey, look! There's the fort!" He sounded so excited that Sophie had to smile.

"We seem to be on the right street, at least," she said. "There's the water but, unless we've missed a turn somewhere, I don't see much of a beach." There were scores of boats bobbing at anchor, and she could see the lights of a bridge just ahead but no sand. No dunes. No sea oats. "I don't understand. I distinctly asked for something right on the beach, but as close as possible to the things you're interested in seeing."

The Hotel de Aviles appeared to be more of a motel than a hotel, and Fate claimed the single remaining parking space. "We'll sort it out in the morning, okay? Sit tight and let me get us checked in, and I'll find out where the nearest decent restaurant is."

The thought of food was enough to overcome her disappointment, and Sophie began gathering up her purse, her cotton cardigan and the map. Fate was right—at the moment, food and a comfortable bed took precedence over all else. She'd worry about finding herself a beach tomorrow.

He was back within minutes. "I'm pretty sure the desk clerk had second thoughts about letting a room to any guy who smelled like a two-bit—uh, flower garden," he confessed with wry grin. "I must be getting used to it. I'd almost forgotten the way I smelled."

Sophie let herself out and took inventory of her surroundings while Fate unloaded the bags. The two-story complex was built in a horseshoe shape that opened onto a narrow street. Directly on the other side of the street, separated only by a sidewalk and a strip of grass, was the water, sparkling with the lights of moored sailboats, a nearby bridge and, most important of all, a restaurant.

The restaurant, built on a pier, was within easy walking distance. Sophie felt her stomach rumble, and she reached for her bag, eager to stash it in her room and go in search of dinner.

"We're on the second floor. I'll bring these," Fate said, striding off toward the staircase. Sophie hurried to keep up. She was not used to having anyone carry her burdens, but she certainly wasn't going to argue about it. "We're on the Matanzas River," he informed her, pausing to unlock her door. "The bridge we just passed leads out to the ocean beach area, but I'm afraid the clerk didn't hold out much hope of our finding a vacancy there on a holiday weekend."

Sophie hid her disappointment as Fate switched on the lights and carried her bag to the luggage rack. The room looked comfortable and clean, and technically speaking, it *was* on the water. There was also a convenient restaurant, she thought, her spirits lifting. "This will do nicely."

Nicely? It was marvelous! It was beautiful! A bed the size of a football field, a palm tree outside her door, and an air conditioner that really worked!

"Well...I guess that's it," she said brightly. Her smile wavered only a little when it occurred to her that for the first time in six years she was standing in the middle of a bedroom with a man. The thought alone was enough to give her a distinctly funny feeling, as if someone had run a finger down her spine.

Dammit, she'd thought that part of her life was safely a thing of the past! Evidently her mind had failed to pass the message along to her body.

"Will ten minutes be enough time?" Fate inquired.

"For what?"

"I thought we'd try the place across the street tonight. I don't know about you, but I'm ready for dinner."

In her weakened condition, there was no way Sophie could turn down an invitation like that. "Could we possibly make that five?"

Whether by luck, bribery, or sheer intimidation, Fate managed to secure them a table almost immediately. Not only that, they had a view. As famished as she was, Sophie was torn between the enticing menu and the equally enticing sight of a full orange moon rising over a calm, broad body of water.

"Have you ever seen anything so lovely? Look! There's a sailboat completely silhouetted against the... Oooh, what's that delicious aroma?" Her head swiveled around as her gaze followed the tray that was being borne past them to the next table. She sighed longingly. "This is too much. I can't believe I'm actually here."

They ordered and then Sophie divided her attention between the view and the other diners. The couple at the next table were Oriental, the woman strikingly beautiful. Just beyond them were a young couple who were so obviously in love that two enormous lobster dinners were being allowed to grow cold.

Personally, Fate was far more interested in the woman seated across the table from him than in his surroundings. The change in her was incredible. From the way she was acting you'd think she'd never been out of Turbyville. If he'd ever known such a provincial woman before, she'd made damned sure no one else knew it. Sophie's lack of pretense was refreshing.

It was also more than a little disconcerting, as it was giving rise to all sorts of emotions he had no business feeling.

In fact, ever since that evening when he'd dropped into the office and found her bent double, her face flushed and her hair all tousled, he'd been harboring some pretty unhealthy ideas. Then he'd gone to her house the morning after the auction and seen her all sprawled out there at his feet, and he'd practically blown his main switch trying to get his mind back on track.

He didn't *want* to think of Sophie Pennybaker as a woman. He needed her too much as a secretary. Besides, he wasn't ready to get involved with any woman, and if and when he changed his mind, he sure as hell wouldn't be looking for someone like Sophie.

Okay, so the thing to do was to get himself organized. Naturally he'd see to it that she had whatever she needed in the way of expense money, transportation, that sort of thing. After that he'd be free to line up his own agenda and cover as much ground as time allowed. With any luck they'd both be too tired for any funny business if they happened to meet back at the motel between activities.

Absently Fate watched as she attacked a platter of shrimp with fork, fingers, and a few appreciative murmurs. For such an inhibited little prude, she showed some remarkably hedonistic tendencies.

Now, where was he—oh, yes. Get Sophie squared away, and then map out a logical plan of attack that would cover as much as possible in as short a time. No telling when he'd have time to take another holiday—he'd better make the most of the time he had.

"If you're not going to eat your last scallop, could I—?" Sophie murmured, her lips glistening with butter.

"Uh—sure! That is, no, of course not—I mean, help yourself." Fate groaned as he felt his grip on reality begin to relax. He tried to tell himself it was all going to work out just as he'd planned, but he was beginning to have some serious doubts.

Six

Outside in the street, a horse clip-clopped past. Sophie had noticed several of the fringed carriages around town and found them enchanting. She sighed in frustration. Two and a half days of complete freedom spread out before her, and what did she do with it? Lie in bed and fantasize about her work. All right, not about work per se, but about her boss, that hard-nosed, cold-eyed creature who'd had every man in the plant sweating within days of his arrival.

And every woman panting, she admitted reluctantly.

She must be coming down with something. Here she was for once in her life with time on her hands and no responsibilities, her only obligation to be at the airport in time for her return flight. What was she doing with this golden opportunity? Fantasizing! And doing a lousy job of it, at that. Evidently the side of her brain where fantasies were supposed to be fabricated had never developed properly. She couldn't get past stage one, where he held her in his arms and pressed her tightly against his manly body.

At least that last part was sheer fantasy. He'd held her in his arms, all right, but his manly body, along with her womanly one, had been strapped to their respective seats. Besides, her mind had been occupied with more pressing matters at the time.

But there was nothing more pressing now, and Sophie was acutely aware of the fact that Fate was sleeping in the next room, separated by a single wall. She tried to picture him in bed, wearing...

All she could think of was the stiff, red cotton pajamas Phil had worn on their wedding night. His mother had picked them out, he'd explained, and he hadn't wanted to seem unappreciative. Somehow, Sophie couldn't picture Fate wearing red cotton pajamas. Red silk, perhaps—or maybe just the bottom halves.

Or maybe nothing at all.

With an impatient snort, she rolled over and poked her pillow with a fist. Memories. Fantasies! Imagine Sophie Pennybaker indulging in fantasies about a man. She hadn't done anything so nonproductive in nearly twenty years. Even then her fantasies had centered on a home and a family more than any particular male figure. Those had never quite taken shape in her mind. She'd only known that when he came along, she'd recognize him. He'd be strong and dependable, gentle and kind.

The few boys Sophie had dated before she'd met Phil Pennybaker had fallen short of the mark, but that was hardly surprising. At a time when most girls her age had been whispering about boys and experimenting with padded bras, high heels, and eye shadow, Sophie had already distanced herself from her peers.

Almost unconsciously she'd assumed an air of reserve as a means of self-protection. That it had often been mistaken for snobbishness had hurt at the time, but it had eventually proved a blessing. At least she'd been left with plenty of time to study all through high school. By the time she'd married Phil, she'd already begun taking night courses and had been given her second promotion at KellyCo.

Oh yes, Sophie was a quick learner—always had been. The only thing she'd never quite mastered was dreams. She was a lousy dreamer, and she'd never really got the hang of fantasizing.

A feeling of expectancy brightened her eyes as she pulled aside the draperies and peered outside early the next morning. At least she hadn't dreamed the water, the sailboats, the palm tree and that glorious sun. Even the sky had a tropical look about it. To Sophie's delight, the bridge began to open. She watched a southbound tug pushing two stubby barges chug past, and her imagination was immediately off on another junket, conjuring up far-flung ports and exotic cargos.

Hurriedly, she showered and dressed in white cotton slacks and a yellow camp shirt. Instead of twisting her hair into its usual coil at the back of her head, she tied it back with a colorful scarf. There were no wild-haired Wendys she felt obliged to set an example for, she reminded herself. She could let down her hair, both literally and figuratively.

What was that old saying that had been so popular a few years ago? Let it all hang out? For the next two days, Sophie vowed cheerfully, she was going to let it drag the ground!

She strolled across the street to the restaurant on the pier, only to discover that it didn't serve breakfast. Never mind. There was bound to be a place nearby where she could get coffee and something to sustain her while she went in search of a beach. The streets were already beginning to fill, and most of the people looked pretty well-fed. Sophie found herself smiling at perfect strangers. Like all the other tourists, she craned her neck to peer at crenellated towers as she wandered down narrow, cobblestone streets.

According to Fate, this was the oldest European settlement in the country. Sophie could well believe it; the atmosphere was almost palpable. No wonder he was so eager to explore. If she wasn't afraid he'd think she was manufacturing an excuse just to be with him—and if she didn't have her heart set on spending all her time at the beach—she might have enjoyed exploring, too.

Finding an inviting-looking café, she ordered *huevos rancheros* for the simple reason that she'd never had it before and wasn't entirely sure what it was. To her relief, she loved it! Whoever said Sophie Pennybaker had no sense of adventure?

Her waitress confirmed her suspicion that the ocean was on the far side of Anastasia Island, and Anastasia Island was on the far side of the bridge. Too far to walk, at any rate. Sophie strolled back to the hotel and conferred with the desk clerk on the best mode of transportation. It didn't occur to her to ask to take the car. Fate was paying for all this; she was only along for the ride.

A short while later she found herself standing on the sun-warmed sand of Anastasia State Park Beach, having taken a taxi from the hotel. The sun was shining, the air was incredibly balmy, and she had a whole day with nothing more pressing to worry about than applying sunscreen at suitable intervals.

Fate had evidently still been sleeping when she'd left the hotel, a bit surprising in view of the fact that he was usually at the office hours before anyone else. After nearly four months of fourteen-hour days and six-day weeks, the poor man was probably exhausted. Come to think of it, he'd barely said three words last night over dinner.

When they'd got back to the hotel, Sophie recalled as she lazily stroked the fragrant lotion into one pale thigh, they'd stood outside her door for the longest time. And he'd simply stared at her, as if in seeing her out of context, he couldn't quite remember who she was. Knowing that a familiar face in unfamiliar surroundings sometimes produced that effect, Sophie had put it down to delayed reaction.

Actually it was a rather startling turn of events, being here this way after months of working together. FloBelle was the only one who hadn't seemed surprised at the way things had turned out. She'd practically worn out her deck of playing cards ever since Sophie had told her about the trip, swearing she'd known something was up as soon as she'd seen the traveling card in the same line with the king of spades and the queen of diamonds.

"Why am I wasting time worrying about Fate and FloBelle and a crazy deck of cards?" Impatiently Sophie crammed the sunscreen into her tote. The sun was shining, and she was lying on the beach, and there, only a few feet away, was the ocean. Incredibly blue, fringed with delicate bands of white lace, it was dotted with swimmers, even at this early hour. She dug into her tote again for the paperback book she'd brought along, determined to put Fate out of her mind.

Fate, bare-chested, barefooted, his white jeans still unbelted, stood in the middle of his room and frowned at the note he'd found wedged under his door. "I've gone to the beach for the day. Enjoy your museums. sp."

sp! What had happened to Sophie? Or even S. Pennybaker? Dammit, she wasn't here as his secretary. Was she so hidebound by convention that she couldn't relate to him on any other level? She'd sure as hell related on that plane. He knew the difference between an office machine and a woman, and that was no computer he'd held in his arms!

Throughout the morning, as he followed the pictorial map to the Lightner Museum, Fate found his wintery mood returning. If she'd bothered to ask, he fumed inwardly, he might have liked to spend a few hours at the beach, too. The trouble with Sophie was that she thought she knew everything. She was just too damned efficient for her own good!

Under other circumstances, Fate admitted reluctantly, he could have spent hours browsing among the collection of other people's collections to be found at his first stop, the Lightner. He'd skipped breakfast because he'd been in no mood to eat, and even that reminded him of Sophie. Right from the first she'd been able to look at him and tell when he was running on empty. She'd send someone out for a sandwich and milk and place it before him without a word, and he'd devour it without looking up from his desk.

Actually, that was probably the sum total of his problem, Fate told himself, relieved. He was just hungry. He'd grab a bite and then head for the next stop on his list. A few hours in the company of assorted firearms, rapiers and swords should put him in a more peaceable frame of mind. After the weapons museum he'd head for the fort and plan on spending the rest of the day there.

It was quite late when Sophie eased herself out of the cab and brushed the few grains of sand from the plastic seat. The sun had already disappeared, but the golden afterglow cast a magic over all it touched. She was exhausted, enchanted, and after a day spent splashing through the surf in her own version of swimming, sleeping and reading in the sun—playing ball with several children who'd invaded her few square feet of space, she'd never felt more relaxed in her life.

"Thank you so much for coming back for me, Emilio. I'll let you know about tomorrow, all right?" She'd arranged with the driver to collect her where he'd dropped her off that morning. He'd recommended the beach where he took his own family, and Sophie had found it everything he'd claimed it to be.

"It's about time you got back!"

Sophie, her tote bag thumping her backside as she wearily climbed the stairs, stared at the tall figure looming over her. "Fate? Is something wrong? Has something happened back home?"

"Would you care? You sure as hell didn't waste any time getting out of here this morning. What's the matter. Afraid I might need you for something?" Hearing the sound of his own words, Fate was astounded. That wasn't at all what he'd planned to say, much less the way he'd planned to say it. Turning away, he stalked across the veranda to stare out over the water. "I was just worried about you, that's all," he muttered. Not even to himself did he want to admit the truth. He'd missed her. He'd missed her like the very devil, and it had spoiled his whole day.

"Did you need me, Fate?" Sophie asked. She climbed the few remaining steps, eased the bag from her shoulder, and crossed to where he stood with his back to her, shoulders hunched, hands braced widely apart on the wrought-iron railing. "You had only to let me know," she said quietly. "I thought it was all settled—I'd spend the weekend at the beach, and you'd take in the forts and museums."

He swung around then, and Sophie reeled at the anger that blazed in his eyes. Backed by the palm-framed vista, with the angular planes of his face bathed in the coppery glow of sunset, he might well have been one of the bold explorers who had claimed this very spot for Spain more than four hundred years ago. "It never occurred to you that I might care to be informed as to your plans?" he challenged. "It never occurred to you that I might worry? What if you hadn't come back—what then? Where was I to have started searching? The clerk who was here this morning when you took off won't be back until Tuesday."

Sophie was flabbergasted. "No—I mean it never occurred to me," she said weakly. "I mean... what you said. Fate, why on earth would you worry about me? I told you where I was going, didn't you get my note?"

"Oh, yeah, that masterpiece you shoved under my door before you disappeared. 'Gone to the beach,'" he quoted sarcastically. "*What* beach? *Which* beach? The whole damned state of Florida is wall-to-wall beach!"

Arms crossed over her chest, Sophie dropped down onto a nearby lounge chair. Damp, salty and sandy, she was in no mood to sort out the workings of any man's mind. She wasn't at work now; she didn't have to decipher the indecipherable or comprehend the incomprehensible.

"Fate, I appreciate your concern, but you're not my keeper. I've been looking after myself for more years than I care to remember, so thank you very much, but I don't need you breathing down my neck, yelling at me when I'm too tired to yell back."

"I did not yell! I merely—"

"You merely pounced on me before I could even get up the stairs, accusing me of—of I don't know what!"

"I didn't accuse you of a damned thing, I simply said that in the future, I'd prefer it if you'd do me the courtesy of informing me of your whereabouts."

Sophie flowed to her feet in a single motion, which brought her practically toe-to-toe with her adversary. "Courtesy! Look who's talking about courtesy! If you dared treat me this way at work, I'd have you up on charges of—of—harassment!"

Fate leaned forward. Sophie stood her ground. It occurred to her fleetingly that if he'd been a bull, he'd have been pawing the earth. "Harassment?" he inquired softly. "We're talking harassment now? Then maybe I'd better give you some grounds to go on."

Sophie stepped back, her leg struck the edge of the chaise lounge, and then it was too late. Off balance, she was hauled into his arms and pulled hard against his body. The spurious energy lent her by anger drained away, leaving her clinging to him for support.

Support was the last thing on her mind as his lips closed over hers, twisting to gain entry to the softness she struggled to deny him. It was all wrong—it was too soon—it was too much! Sophie tried desperately to think of all the reasons why she should fight against what was happening, and then she stopped thinking altogether. Senses came into play, senses newly alive, wildly intoxicating. The taste of him was like nothing she'd ever experienced—sweet and fresh, and excitingly male. She'd spread her hands on his chest in instinctive protest, but already they were moving over the thin knit of his shirt, discovering the planes, shapes and textures of his body, sliding daringly into the hidden warmth beneath his arms.

Fate held her close, cupping the back of her head with one hand while the other moved slowly down her spine toward her waist... and below. Sophie, her skin sensitized by hours in the sun, muscles tired from hours in the surf, felt as if every raw nerve in her body was exposed. Half-forgotten urges stirred to life, confusing her still further.

Nor was Fate unaffected. As he lovingly explored the hidden darkness behind her lips with his tongue, his body was reacting in ways that were unmistakable.

Alarm bells began to sound somewhere in the back of Sophie's mind. *Wind chimes,* a small voice whispered. *Ignore them.* Fate lifted his mouth from hers and his lips moved slowly to the hollow behind her ear, the heat of his breath setting free the mingled fragrance of sunscreen and sea. She shuddered uncontrollably. A sweet, burgeoning ache had settled in the lower part of her body, arousing memories of...

This absolutely had to stop right now, she told herself firmly. Then Fate buried his face in the hollow of her throat, and she groaned, her knees buckling so that she could hardly stand. "This has simply got to stop," she managed to whisper.

Fate said nothing. His hands were engaged in a roundabout tour that would lead to her breasts unless she called a halt right now. Evidently he'd showered recently, for his hair was still damp, and he smelled of soap and some subtle masculine scent that could easily incite a riot in any gathering of two or more women.

"Fate, that's enough," she gasped, wrenching herself from his arms. "If this is your idea of a joke, I don't find it particularly funny. And now, if you don't mind, I'm going to get out of these sticky clothes and go out for dinner."

"Alone?"

She nodded, not trusting herself to speak. Obviously her judgment wasn't the only thing impaired by too much sun and saltwater—her voice had sounded about as convincing as the roar of a paper dragon.

"I'd like to go with you."

"I don't think that's a very good idea. Look, Fate, we both went along with the auction because it was for a good cause. But just because I bought you—or won you. Or whatever... Oh, you know what I mean!" she cried, confused and hating it. "There's just no reason at all to pretend any longer. Petra George isn't around to take notes. As far as Turbyville and the Dunwoody Committee knows, we've each fulfilled our part of the bargain."

"And that's it? The fact that we're friends, that we happen to be staying in the same hotel in a strange city doesn't mean a thing to you?"

"But we *aren't* friends," Sophie exclaimed. "We're employer and employee. I *work* for you, and I don't make a habit of socializing with people I work for. It's bad policy."

Arms crossed over his chest, jaw thrust forward, Fate stared at her morosely. How many times had he repeated those very words? And he'd meant them, too. Yet how irrelevant they seemed at this moment. Dammit, he *wanted* to socialize with Sophie Pennybaker. He wanted more than that—a hell of a lot more!

Suddenly his good humor seemed restored. The crooked half smile that deepened the groove in his cheek was back. "All right, Sophie, we'll go our separate ways—at least for tonight. As for tomorrow, I'd like to get in a couple of hours at a beach while I'm here. Maybe you could recommend one?"

Warily, Sophie told him about the state park beach where she'd spent the day. "I understand there's another public beach at the other end of Anastasia Island. I thought I might try that tomorrow."

"How did you plan on traveling?"

"The driver who took me today gave me his card. I promised to call him if I wanted to go anywhere."

Fate's lips tightened imperceptibly. "Did it ever occur to you to take the car?"

"No," she said simply.

"We may as well drive. Then if this new beach doesn't pan out, we can always go back to the place you went today."

There was no way she could justify a refusal. Sophie nodded, picked up the tote she'd dropped and turned toward her door. "Would about nine suit you, or is that too early?"

"No, that's fine."

He didn't offer to unlock her door, but Sophie was conscious of his gaze burning through the back of her damp beach wrap, making her unusually clumsy as she fumbled the key, dropped her purse, and bumped her knee on the doorjamb. Her Serene Highness, the cool, unflappable Mrs. Pennybaker, she thought with a wry stab of amusement. What a shining example *she'd* turned out to be.

She'd just stepped out from under the shower, her hair dripping down her back, when someone rapped on her door. It could only be Fate or maid service, and she already had plenty of towels. She was tempted to ignore it, but if it was Fate, he'd either rupture his knuckles or bring the management down on their heads before he'd give up.

"All right, I'm coming," she called out impatiently, tugging her beach wrap on over her wet and naked body. It hadn't occurred to her to pack a bathrobe. What did she know about packing?

"Hey, did I get you out of the tub?" Fate inquired with patently false concern. "I'm sorry, Sophie. I should've called."

"What do you want?" she demanded, tight-lipped.

It was the wrong question to ask under the circumstances, with wet patches blooming wherever skin touched the soft cotton fabric. Fate's eyes dropped to her breasts, and she felt their response as clearly as if he'd touched her. Her hand shifted to slam the door, but his reflexes were faster.

Wedging a foot into the opening, he said, "You'll catch cold if you don't get into something warm and dry. What I wanted to ask was, do you know of a good place to have breakfast?"

Hiding behind the door, Sophie frowned at him. "Couldn't you have waited to ask me that?"

"I suppose I could, but since we probably won't be seeing each other again tonight, and I don't want to miss breakfast again tomorrow, I thought—" He paused, and Sophie waited. The cold blast from the air conditioner was hitting her squarely on her wet fanny. She started to speak, but he shushed her. "Wait. I thought I heard my phone ringing. Did you hear anything?"

"No, I didn't hear anything, but as for breakfast, there's a—"

Fate interrupted her. "I'm pretty sure it's my phone. Look, I'd better run. I'll catch you later and you can tell me about this place, okay?"

Twenty minutes later, Sophie let herself out. Somehow, she wasn't at all surprised when the dark shape that separated itself from the shadow of the palm tree turned out to be Fate.

"Where had you planned on having dinner, at the place across the street?"

Sophie nodded and started down the stairs. He was right behind her. "About the breakfast place," she began when he broke in.

"Don't even mention food until I get within range of a seafood platter. I sort of missed out on lunch, too."

"Good heavens, you're the one who needs a keeper," Sophie said shortly.

Adjusting his stride to accommodate her shorter one, Fate smiled slowly, his eyes kindling with a distinctly challenging gleam. Wasn't that just what he'd been trying to tell her?

Seven

Sophie permitted herself to be escorted across the street to the restaurant. At the door, she halted, turning to Fate. "You're under no obligation to feed me," she felt compelled to say.

"Technically I believe I am. Although I don't consider it an obligation. More of a privilege. That sounds like a lousy line, doesn't it?" he added with a sparkle of amusement.

"Definitely a line, but not lousy—just rather unimaginative." Sophie did her best to ignore the all too familiar tug of desire as she brushed past him through the door. Dammit, he had no business flashing his dimple at her when she was trying to put him in his place. Fate at his worst was bad enough; at his best he was lethal!

"Tell me, Sophie, what would you consider an imaginative line?" he asked softly as they were being led to a table overlooking the bridge. "I've been out of action for so long I must be getting rusty."

"Oh, knock it off, Ridgeway," Sophie muttered, amused in spite of herself. "We both know I probably wouldn't recognize a line if I tripped over one. Are you having seafood again tonight, or did all those forts and cannons put you in a red meat frame of mind?"

"Women," he said in mock disgust. "They never understand men's interest in hardware."

But they both ordered the seafood, and then Fate began telling her about the places he'd visited that day. "My father was in the foundry business—engine blocks, gears and gear boxes, that sort of thing," he explained. "One Christmas he gave me a set of lead soldiers that had belonged to his father. They were beautifully cast—two armies, fully equipped. The detailing was unbelievable. Mom raised hell with him for trusting a kid with something like that."

"War toys, antiques or lead?"

"All of the above, but mostly it was the war part. She was a militant peacemonger in those days. She really pitched a fit when Dad starting casting replicas of all those old armaments, claimed he was fostering the fighting urge in his only son." He chuckled, a sound Sophie found completely entrancing. "All it fostered was an abiding interest in history, actually. I wanted to major in it, but Dad was counting on my taking over the foundry and Mom was afraid I'd die a pauper with my head in the clouds. She didn't have a lot of use for what she termed fuzzy-headed dreamers—the ivory-tower set."

"I can't imagine any less likely description of you."

"Ah, but that's because I got a solid bankable education in math, engineering and business administration. No pipe, tweeds and elbow patches for me."

"Evidently it was a wise decision. Look at you now—comptroller of an international corporation, flying all over the world to sort out their affairs."

"Yes, but where's the romance in spreadsheets and profit-loss statements?" He leaned forward, chin resting on his fists, eyes dancing. "Maybe if we put the workers in uniform, something in red, white and blue, with stovepipe collars, bandoliers, and lots of gold braid for the top management..."

Sophie giggled, and Fate grinned. They both sighed and found their eyes meeting and clinging.

Relaxed by wine and good food, it was impossible not to drift deeper into the comfortable intimacy that had sprung up so unexpectedly between them. Fate shifted condiments about on the table as if they were opposing armies, and Sophie watched his hands, admiring their strength, their grace, their control. "I was about ten when Dad first began casting the occasional replica for a museum or a historical site. When I was fourteen he got an order for five fifteenth-century Spanish cannons and eight block-mounted swivel guns. He took me with him on a research trip to Madrid, and I really got the bug then."

"Where are your parents now?" Sophie prompted gently.

"Dad died fourteen years ago, a few months after the foundry shut down. Mother sold the house and moved in with her younger sister in New Jersey. I think she still blames Dad for losing the business on account of a silly hobby of his, but the truth is, the market was already changing. Like too many other businesses, the foundry couldn't compete in a global economy, and so it went under."

Sophie listened attentively, hoping he'd go on talking. The more she knew about him, the more of a threat he was to her peace of mind, yet she didn't want him to stop. She was reluctantly coming to realize that everything about the man fascinated her.

"Sorry for monopolizing the conversation," Fate said with a faintly embarrassed look. "Or do I mean monotonizing it?"

"Don't be ridiculous, I'm interested. It never occurred to me to wonder who made all those cannons and things you see in public parks. I guess I just assumed they were the real thing."

"Some are, most aren't. Most of the remaining authentic ones are snapped up by collectors and museums."

"With your interest in history, I can understand why you put together this particular date package for the auction."

"Pretty selfish, huh?" He grinned sheepishly.

"Not really. Not at all, in fact. I happen to know that the man who auctioned off a cruise to Bimini would rather fish for marlin than eat when he's hungry. And Ralph Anstey, the man who auctioned off that weekend in Las Vegas? Do you honestly think he hates gambling?"

"Point taken," Fate said with a grin. "You're good, Mrs. Pennybaker. I can see why you're considered such an oracle around Turbyville."

Sophie almost strangled over that remark. "You're confusing me with FloBelle—she's the Pennybaker with all the answers. I know precisely what my reputation is, and believe me, there's nothing oracular about it," she said, amused. "If the women at KellyCo sometimes come to me with their problems, it's only because I've been there so long. I know the ropes."

"And the men?"

"You mean do I know them, or do they come to me with their problems?" Her smile was gently teasing, and Fate found himself totally captivated by the slightest overlapping of her front teeth. "Look, do we have to talk about KellyCo? There's only one full day of my holiday left, and I don't intend to waste a second of it."

"*Our* holiday," Fate corrected gently. However, she was right about one thing—there was no time to waste. Frowning slightly, he considered the options. It was going to require delicacy as well as precision. It hadn't taken him long to realize that Sophie was not a woman to be rushed. He'd seen her drop more than one poor devil in his tracks with a few polite words. Most of those who'd been around for a while knew better than to try anything.

"Now you know all about my secret affair with lead soldiers, what do you do for relaxation, Sophie?"

"I gave away my doll when I was thirteen. Now I'm hooked on old books. Not necessarily classics, just old ones. Fiction, nonfiction, anything. The how-to's around the turn of the century are fascinating. Would you believe preserving a winter's supply of eggs by floating them in a barrel of lime water? Or making your own tooth powder with charcoal, soda and oil of peppermint? And the fiction—it's like stepping back in time."

Well, I'll be damned, thought Fate. So she likes history, too, and she doesn't even know it. "That's it? You read?"

"I also watch birds. And I cook. There's always something that needs doing around the house, if I get bored with all that. Last spring I painted it."

Great. So she was a paragon at home, as well as at work. If he weren't so damned intrigued, he might even be intimidated. "What about this FloBelle character? What does she do?" If he couldn't get to her using the direct route, there was always the flank attack.

"Phil's mother? She gardens—herbs and wildflowers, mostly. She brews things with the herbs, and reads the leaves in the bottom of teacups. And astrology—she does that. And psychometry. Sometimes she and her friends sit around a table and—uh, commune. She's really a remarkable woman."

Remarkable was one way of putting it. He'd heard less charitable descriptions from his landlady, who knew everything about everybody, and considered it her duty to pass it on. "How'd you end up living with your ex-husband's mother, anyway? Isn't that a pretty unusual setup?"

Sophie shrugged. "I shouldn't think so. We were both alone. Flo needed someone to... well, to keep an eye on her. She's not terribly practical, you know. She really didn't have anyone but me, and I was glad of the company."

"I take it your divorce was an amicable one?" It was a leading question, and they both knew it.

Sophie gave him a level look. "Fate, I'm sure that by now you've been briefed on all the town's gossip. Phil and I are stale news. That happened six years ago."

"*What* happened six years ago?" he probed gently, his wintergreen eyes more compelling than eyes had a right to be.

"Phil left me." Dammit, he'd probably heard it all anyway; she might as well replace whatever version he'd been fed by that nosy landlady of his with the rather dull official one. "We'd been married for nine years, and we got along reasonably well, and one day Phil went out on his route and kept on going. End of story. It really wasn't very exciting, so you can forget all the bizarre versions you've no doubt heard. I've heard most of them, too—I've even laughed at some of the more creative ones."

Fate had an idea she hadn't done much laughin' at the time. It hadn't taken him very long to learn that minding one's neighbor's business was a full-time occupation in an underemployed town where gossip was endemic. God, how she must've hurt, a woman as proud and private as his Sophie, having to endure all the speculation. Even in the urban circles he moved in, when a man simply walked out on his family without warning, there was talk. He'd heard three versions of Sophie's story already, none of them even faintly credible.

"We've been divorced for years now. Phil's since remarried, quite happily, I believe. He's a nice man, and I'm fond of FloBelle. She may strike some people as strange, but it's only because she doesn't see things the way most of us do. She sees only the good in people, and that has a way of bringing out the best in everyone. Flo's theory is that you create your own reality. Sometimes I wonder if she's not right."

"Hmmm," Fate murmured noncommittally. "I'll take your word for it." But his mind wasn't on the woman who'd risen up out of a bed of weeds in a purple shroud to ask him when he was born. He was far more interested in a woman who felt responsible for the mother of a man who'd deserted her.

Deserted her! What kind of fool would desert a woman like Sophie after he'd been lucky enough to win her? Viewing the matter objectively—an increasingly difficult task, Fate was coming to realize—he'd probably known more beautiful women. But none with Sophie's unique blend of strength and vulnerability, of integrity and loyalty. Not to mention her plain damned skittishness, he added—objectively.

He allowed his gaze to linger on her eyes, which were the color of wood smoke, but as clear as rainwater, before moving on to the short, straight nose that had turned faintly pink after a day at the beach. And to her mouth. He shifted restlessly in his seat. Just the sight of her mouth, as soft and sweet as a whisper in the night, brought an uncomfortable tightening to his groin.

She was talking. Damn! He'd been so distracted just looking at her he'd missed half of what she was saying.

"His name's Emilio, and he has four sons and three daughters, and he wants to own his own tour company someday after his children are grown."

Fate reconstructed quickly, realizing that she was referring to the taxi driver who'd dropped her off at the hotel. "For someone who's been known to cut a man dead for asking her out to dinner, you sure didn't waste much time buddying up to this guy, did you?"

"That's not true," she protested. "Well, perhaps at work, I do tend to be more reserved—"

"Refrigerated." He was teasing, but not really. Who the hell was this Emilio guy, anyway?

"I beg your pardon?"

"I've seen frost dripping off a man's ears after a few words with you. Remember the first time I asked you out? I was new in town, I asked you out to dinner—no big deal, just a meal, maybe a few drinks and a little friendly conversation. You bit my head off, and for the rest of that week, the temperature in the office was about ten degrees below normal."

"That's not true," Sophie protested quickly. "I simply said no thank you."

Fate's eyes glinted with amusement. To tell the truth, he'd been relieved at the time. He'd had to try. No man could be around a woman like Sophie for any length of time without trying his luck, but he'd always considered it a major mistake to get involved with a woman who worked for him.

However, in Sophie's case, he'd have made an exception.

Exception, hell! He'd known in his bones almost from the very first day that the tension he'd felt everytime she'd come within five feet of him hadn't been entirely one-sided. He'd also known that it was apt to get a whole lot worse before it got better. Agreeing to go along with this auction thing, and then rigging it the way he had, had probably been a subconscious move on his part to get her away from the office, where they could explore this thing and discover how deep it went.

Unfortunately before he even realized what was happening it had already gone far deeper than he'd intended, and he still wasn't anywhere close to understanding it.

Sophie blotted her lips, and he envied the napkin. "Fate, I can't help it if I happen to be reserved," she said. "It's just my nature."

"Mine," he said in a tone that was unmistakable in its intent, "is to go after what I want. And right now, Mrs. Pennybaker, I think you know what that is."

They left the restaurant and in silent agreement, turned to walk along the lighted sidewalk that bordered the river. There was a small park with games and a bandstand, several piers, a few benches nestled amidst fragrant patches of garden and sheltered from the streetlight by overhanging branches.

They avoided them like the plague. The raw awareness between them was still too powerful. Until they brought it under control Sophie preferred to walk, and for once she took the lead. "Shall we tackle the bridge? Looks like a nice climb."

It was. They walked all the way to the other side, with Sophie hurrying over the center portion, with its four towers, in case it began to swing open under her feet.

The sidewalk was narrow. On the way back, her hand kept brushing against Fate's thigh, until he captured it and held on. Sophie's knees almost buckled under the physical assault that slammed into her body. *He's just holding your hand, you idiot! A perfectly harmless, rather sophomoric pastime—certainly nothing to get all hot and bothered about.*

She waited for him to release her hand while she struggled to get her breathing under control. Her palm was sweating—oh, how awful! What if he was tired of holding hands, but afraid to let go for fear of offending her? Men like Fate Ridgeway didn't hold hands, for pity's sake. He'd probably been tired of her bumping against his thigh... his hard, muscular thigh.

Oh, heavens!

Never had silence been filled with so many voices, Sophie thought as they climbed the stairs back at the hotel. With the cadence of a horse-drawn carriage and her own pounding heart as background, Sophie argued with herself about whether or not to ask him inside. If he came in, he'd kiss her, and if he kissed her, there was no way she could stop him if he wanted to make love to her, because she wanted it, too. More than anything she'd ever wanted in her entire life, she wanted Fate Ridgeway. In every way there was.

A soft sound of dismay escaped her.

Fate removed the key from her limp and useless hand. "What did you say, Sophie?"

"Oh, um—I said, thank you for dinner. And the walk. It was very enjoyable."

"Mr. Ridgeway."

"What?" Puzzled, she stared up at his moon-shadowed face.

"You forgot to add the Mr. Ridgeway part to your frosty little bread-and-butter speech."

"I did?" she repeated, mesmerized. "Oh. You're teasing me."

Fate put the key in her lock and then imprisoned her against the door, an arm on either side of her shoulders. "Yes, Sophie, I'm teasing you. Because if I don't tease you now, I'll be making love to you in a very short time, and I'm not sure you're ready for that. Are you?" he asked, his voice a husky aphrodisiac.

She pressed against the door, weak with a desire that had been held under control for too long. Ready? She'd never been more ready for anything in her life, but if he had to ask, then perhaps he was the one who wasn't ready.

Sophie averted her face and began exerting every shred of willpower she possessed. He was absolutely right, she told herself. It would be a mistake they'd both regret afterwards. How could she even consider jeopardizing a lifetime of hard-earned security for one brief moment of bliss?

Besides, what made her think there'd even *be* a moment of bliss? For either of them?

Which made it all the more impossible. If the man who'd cared enough for her to marry her hadn't been able to make love to her, how could she even consider offering herself to a man she loved as much as she loved Fate Ridgeway?

She loved Fate Ridgeway? She couldn't possibly! She didn't even know the man. Besides, she had far better sense than to fall in love with—

"Sophie! Come back from wherever you've gone, darling. Let me say good-night to you while I can still let you go."

He kissed her then. Slowly and carefully, as if offering her a chance to escape. Sophie's lips parted hungrily, and she wrapped her arms around his waist. Dammit, she didn't want to be let go!

It was the same old story all over again. Phil had finally come right out and told her that she was just one of those overpowering women who insisted on giving more than a man wanted to accept. She'd vowed at the time *never* to put herself in such a humiliating position again. So here she was—right back in the same miserable old boat, only this time it was even worse. This time the man was Fate.

He was barely able to keep from pushing her away; she could feel the strain in every quivering muscle. Even as he kissed her, his firm, moist lips touching, lifting, and touching again, she could sense his reluctance, and she could have wept. "I'm sorry, I—"

That was as far as she got. His mouth ground into hers, and it was as if a dam had broken. Sophie hung on, her mind in chaos, her senses reeling as he kissed her eyelids, her nose, the corners of her mouth. She felt the tip of his tongue ream the shallow dimple in her chin, and then he took her lips again. There were no tentative overtures this time. It was a hard kiss, almost ruthless in its intensity. His tongue forced its way past her lips, demanding a response that had been his for the asking. Demanding what she'd offered freely.

He cupped her breast in his hand, and she leaned into his palm, feeling her flesh tightening to his touch. Sensations like none she'd ever experienced before telegraphed their way through her body, hammering out messages of fire, flood, and massive upheavals.

Her clothes were sticking to her body, and she wanted to throw them off, tear away anything that could possibly come between her body and his.

But not here. "Fate, I think we'd better go inside," she said weakly. He was leaning against her, every sinew and muscle of his hard body pressed tightly against her, promising a fulfillment she'd waited a lifetime to experience.

"Sophie, are you sure this is right for you?" he whispered hoarsely.

"Please, Fate—I'm sure." What kind of man would ask a question like that at a time like this? Was he trying to back out without hurting her feelings? Was she doing it again, coming on too strong?

His hand moved around behind her and he opened the door. "I only want you to be sure, Sophie," he said as he guided her inside the room. "If you'd rather not rush into anything, I can handle that. I might spend the rest of the weekend under a cold shower, but I can handle it."

His laughter didn't quite come off, but it went a long way toward relieving Sophie's anxiety. In the process, it also banked the fires of passion sufficiently for her to consider what it would mean if they made love together. Fate had said nothing at all about loving her. He was only in Turbyville until someone else came down to take over. Could she handle having an affair with him, knowing it couldn't last? Far better, she told herself candidly, than she could handle loving him and *not* taking what he offered. It would hurt when he went away, but she was no stranger to the pain of being left behind. She'd cut her teeth on it.

"I think," she said calmly, "if it's all right with you, I would like to sleep with you."

Fate moved in front of her and took her face between his hands, gazing down at her with an intensity that, if he but knew it, branded her his for life. "Sleep, Sophie?" he queried gently.

She smiled, although her chin felt a disconcerting tendency to wobble. "A euphemism. You're a man of the world—you know what I mean."

"Believe me, my small-town princess, I'm not the man of the world you seem to think." He laughed softly, letting his hands move down her shoulders, and then to the buttons on the front of her dress. "But I'll do my best not to disappoint you."

By the time she was standing before him in only her bra and panties, dainty scraps of pink satin and ecru lace, Sophie was trembling all over. Her mouth was dry, her palms were damp, and she desperately wanted to dive under the bedspread and cover herself, head and all. Her legs were too long. She was too thin. Her stomach wasn't quite flat, and her breasts were too full for the rest of her body. She had freckles on her shoulders and on her back.

Oh, please make him want me, she thought fervently. Make him think I'm desirable, and not too forward.

"Sweet Sophie, are you going to stand there scowling at me all night, or are you going to help me undress?" Fate asked, a whimsical smile on his face.

"I'm going to—do you really want me to help you? Fate, am I—?"

"Are you what?" he asked gently, peeling off his shirt and reaching for his buckle.

"You know." She couldn't quite meet his eyes. "Am I all right?"

He whipped off his belt, unzipped his fly, and stepped out of his pants before he answered her. Then he gathered her in his arms and lowered her to the bed, rolling onto his elbows so that he was gazing down at her. "All right? Are you *all right*? No, darling, you're not all right." He took her small chin between his teeth and tickled it with the tip of his tongue. "You're perfect. If you'd had the body of a cow and a face like the grill of a Mack truck, I might've had a few second thoughts about taking you to bed, but lucky for me, you turned out to be halfway decent." His voice roughened. "In fact, I'd venture to say you're about the most halfway-decent woman I've seen in my whole life, and that includes centerfolds."

Was she all right, Fate thought wonderingly. If any other woman had asked him that, he'd have sworn she was fishing, but not Sophie. Not this paragon, this frozen confection he'd lusted after and depended on since the second time he'd set eyes on her.

"Sophie, before I surrender the last ounce of judgment I possess, I think I'd better tell you that I—uh, didn't exactly come dressed for the party. By that I mean I wasn't expecting—uh, the occasion to arise." It had arisen, though. Had it ever!

"You mean—? Oh." Her face flamed, and she averted her eyes. "I'm afraid I'm not—uh, dressed, either."

Fate took her face between his hands until she met his gaze. He was shaken by the wave of tenderness that swept over him at her hesitant confession. "There are other ways, darling. I promise you, it'll be all right."

With the urgency of his need pulsing against her, Sophie found it almost impossible to speak. "There are?" she murmured. "I mean, of course there are."

There were? She felt incredibly stupid. After nine years of marriage, she was supposed to know about these things. How could she tell him she knew less than most teenagers, because she'd been too embarrassed to buy "that sort of book" before she was married, knowing how people talked. And after she was married, they'd have wondered why she needed it. Life in a goldfish bowl didn't offer a lot in the way of sex education, at least not for a woman in her situation. She'd always been much too reserved to discuss her intimate concerns with any of the women she knew.

Fate brushed his lips over hers, teasingly at first. She was lying on her back, arms at her sides, afraid to make a move for fear it would be the wrong one.

"Touch me, Sophie," he whispered against her throat, and she squirmed as lightning streaked through her body, finding the direct route to the most surprising places.

"How? I mean how do you like to be... touched?"

Instead of telling her, he showed her, taking her hand and placing it on his chest. Her fingers curled into the thicket of dark hair she found there, inadvertently touching one of his nipples, and she felt his manhood thrust against her thigh. So far, so good, she thought with a wild surge of delight. I can't be a total washout, not when he—*Ahhh...*

Fate had managed to remove her bra and his tongue was toying with the sensitive tips of her breasts. Greatly daring, Sophie ran her hand over his back, dragging her fingernails as far as she could reach down the valley of his spine. As her hands neared the taut flare of his buttocks, the flesh grew silky and cool to her touch, and she wriggled beneath him in order to reach more of him.

More wriggling. The few remaining scraps of clothing were discarded, and then Fate began a tour of discovery, caressing places so exquisitely sensitive that she cried out, kissing her in ways she'd never dreamed of before.

All the while, he murmured words of encouragement, of appreciation, as her own forays grew more daring. "Please, Fate, can't we—?" she pleaded when the ache inside her grew intolerable.

"Darling, we can wait until tomorrow. I'm in no shape to go hunt up a drugstore at this time of night. I'd get picked up for DWI before I got half a block."

"I need to feel you inside me," she cried softly.

Fate groaned. He'd have bartered his soul to give her what she wanted—what they both wanted—but for her sake, he didn't dare. Not with Sophie. She was too dear to him to risk hurting.

Holding her tightly, he covered her mouth with his, setting up a rhythm with his tongue that had her moving restlessly beneath him. Then, using all the skill at his command, plus a tenderness he'd never come close to feeling before, he sought out the hidden secrets of her womanhood, delving, caressing, stroking until she began to grow tense in his arms. She gasped, stiffened, and shuddered, arching wildly as she found release. Fate's smile as he absorbed her soft cries into his heart was more a grimace, but it, too, held satisfaction of a sort.

He turned away, not quite trusting his control. Moments passed and then he felt her move against his back and slip her arms around his waist. "Fate? Are you all right? I'm sorry if I embarrassed you."

Embarrassed him! He felt almost like lashing out at her, but he managed to control that urge, as well. Frustration might be great for building character, but it was hell on the nerves.

"Honey, you didn't embarrass me," he said gruffly. "I'm just—under a bit of pressure at the moment. You can understand that, I presume?"

She grew still at that. He could hear the slight catch of her breath, and he cursed himself for an insensitive jerk. So she'd gone off like a rocket, and he was lying here with a burning fuse, was that any reason to take it out on her? She'd offered, and in an attack of nobility, he'd turned her down.

Maybe he'd go find an all-night racketball court.

"Fate, can't I please help you?" Her voice was so low it was barely audible over the hum of the air conditioner. "The way you helped me, I mean—or any way you want me to. I just—I'm sorry if I seem stupid and—and selfish." She forced a small laugh, and the sound nearly tore him apart. "I'm afraid you'll have to show me, though. I'm not too good at this sort of thing."

He turned to her then, gathering her in his arms to bury his face against her hair. "Ah, Sophie, Sophie, where have you been all your life? That sounds like another line, doesn't it?"

"I think the line goes more like 'where have you been all *my* life?'"

"Where have you?" he asked, stroking her back until she was perfectly aligned with his body.

"That's a short, dull story, and I can think of far more interesting ways to spend the rest of our holiday, can't you?"

He could. The moon was already sinking in the west before they finally fell asleep in each other's arms, sated with pleasure, separated only by their private concerns for the future.

Eight

Fate loped along the river's edge, his long legs eating up the distance as he turned off onto the bridge. Nearing the apex, he slackened his pace, momentarily distracted by the drama of soft purple darkness giving way to gray pearl dawn.

A layer of mist drifted just over the water, shrouding the base of the bridge. The pungent smell of ocean and river mingled pleasantly with the heavy sweetness of some unfamiliar flower. Muffled sounds drifted across the water from a nearby pier. Someone was frying bacon. The total ambience was earthy, mysterious, and oddly cheerful.

Fate had left Sophie sleeping, slipped next door to his own room to shower, and then stood on the veranda watching the eastern sky grow warm with a promise of light. He hadn't gone back inside, knowing that if he did, there'd be no leaving—at least, not until hunger of another sort drove them out in search of breakfast. They were booked on an 11:00 a.m. flight the next day, which meant that regardless of what happened today, they'd be together for the drive to Jacksonville and the flight home. Sooner or later they had to talk, but before they did, he had some serious thinking to do. Before it was too late.

All right, so he'd slept with her last night. They were both responsible, consenting adults. Where was the problem?

He ransacked his brain for an answer as his feet pounded softly over the bridge. The problem was that Sophie Pennybaker was raising merry hell with his libido to the point where it was beginning to affect his judgment.

Beginning! He was already so screwed up in his thinking he even found himself contemplating the big *M*.! Fate Ridgeway—erstwhile playboy, dedicated workaholic—in other words, the quintessential bachelor. His knack for gracefully sidestepping the issue of marriage had made him the envy of all his unmarried acquaintances.

The male ones, at least.

Then along came Sophie. Hell, he hadn't even worried about her. As attractive as she was, he'd never once considered her a serious threat to his freedom. Obviously he'd forgotten all the history he'd ever known. Here was a prime example of Trojan horse strategy, and he hadn't even recognized it.

Or was it a case of the tortoise and the hare?

Okay, so maybe—just *maybe*—he'd had some vague notion of spending a weekend with Sophie without the whole town's keeping score. He hadn't instigated the damned auction, he told himself self-righteously. He'd even resisted at first. His main reason for giving in was that it seemed like a worthwhile cause, and besides, they'd both needed a break.

Okay, so where had he gone wrong? At what point had he lost control of the situation? More important, how was it going to affect Sophie?

Six years was a long time for any woman who'd once been married to sleep alone, yet he'd be willing to swear that she *had* slept alone. Not that it would have mattered to him, Fate assured himself as he jogged the last few yards down the bridge and crossed to the other side for the return.

All right, so it would've mattered. At least he had the grace to be ashamed of feeling that way. And that was just one more indication of how far he'd fallen! Among his own small circle of friends, experience—discreet experience, of course—was not only taken for granted, it was appreciated. On both sides.

But that had been before he'd met Sophie. "Sophie Pennybaker's a right nice girl, I don't care what anybody says." Fate had been informed of that fact by his landlady before he'd even met the secretary that had come with his position as acting Chief Executive Officer. "She's a hard worker and a decent woman, and I for one give her credit for taking in poor foolish Flo-Belle Pennybaker, even if some says she only done it to show up that son o' hers."

All of which had been pretty confusing at the time. It had been some time before he'd found out that the son belonged to poor, foolish FloBelle; much longer before he'd learned the details of the relationship.

Fate put no stock in gossip. In an effort to keep it to a minimum, from the first day he'd arrived on the job, he'd spelled out in advance every policy change, no matter how small, and just how it would affect the employees. He'd formed his own opinions, based on his own observations, and that applied to Sophie as well as every other employee of KellyCo Dye and Finishing.

All the same, he'd have had to be blind not to notice that in spite of the looks of frank masculine appreciation, Sophie was invariably treated by her coworkers with a mixture of respect and affection that spoke for itself. He'd seen more than one clue that she'd managed to cover some high-level blunders before they could do any damage. Smart woman.

Yet, he couldn't quite see her fitting comfortably into his usual life-style. The thought of her living in his Manhattan apartment, sleeping to the sound of a white-noise generator designed to cover the harsher noises of the city, was inconceivable. A woman like Sophie needed wind chimes and pine trees and bird feeders to thrive. Hell, she didn't even lock her door half the time!

"So, my sweet Sophie," he muttered as his soft-soled shoes struck the sidewalk again, "where do we go from here?"

After last night he wanted her so much just thinking about it made his shorts grow uncomfortably tight. She'd been so hesitant, almost as if she were afraid of offending him. Even after she'd turned molten in his arms, she'd still been shy, as if she were embarrassed by the pleasure her body was capable of feeling. Yet she'd given of herself more generously than any woman he'd ever known. "Ah, Sophie," Fate groaned, "what are you doing to me?"

The hotel sign loomed ahead, its dew-wet surface pink in the reflected light of the rising sun. He was no nearer to finding any answers than he'd been when he'd left there and headed along the river toward the old fort. And there were a few things that couldn't wait much longer. His conscience was already putting the squeeze on him.

Mere hours before they'd left town, Fate had had a call from Harry Chamus, informing him that he'd be bringing along his own secretary and asking Fate to scout out a decent apartment for her. Fate had told him about Sophie, extolling her experience and her qualifications, but it seemed that Harry was diabetic. His own secretary had been with him for years, managing his diet as well as his office.

Fate had still been trying to work out a solution that would involve both women when they'd boarded the plane. And then Sophie had heard the wheels retracting, and from that point on, KellyCo and its personnel problems had ceased to exist.

"Good morning. I'm starving, have you had breakfast yet?"

At the sound of her voice, Fate glanced up to see Sophie, chin resting on her crossed arms on the wrought-iron railing. She was seated on the edge of a lounge chair, her expression an enchanting mixture of eagerness, shyness, and wariness.

"Just waiting for you to wake up, sleepyhead," Fate said, his voice husky with unplanned warmth. He thought of the balcony scene in *Romeo and Juliet* and cursed himself for letting things get out of hand with someone as vulnerable as Sophie. If he had a shred of decency, he'd bow out right now, before things went any further.

His pulse rate double-clutched into high gear, and it had nothing to do with his taking the stairs two at a time. Sophie was still smiling when he reached her side, but Fate could see shadows lurking in the clear depths of her eyes.

He slipped his arms around her, rocking her gently from side to side. "I could sure use a kiss about now," he teased, wanting only to erase all the shadows from her eyes—from her life. He nuzzled her shower-sweet neck. "It's been almost five hours since the last one. I'm beginning to feel deprived."

Sophie laughed and lifted her face, hugging his sweat-dampened body enthusiastically. The shadows were gone, he noted with satisfaction a moment later. It had probably been just his imagination.

After a lingering kiss that left his head soaring and his knees like rubber bands, Fate went in to shower and change while Sophie went to her own room to call home. She'd checked in with FloBelle soon after they'd got in, but last night neither of them had been thinking of phone calls home.

Some ten minutes later she let him in again. "Flo must be out in her garden already. Her latest project is drying herbs and wildflowers and sewing them into little sachets for people to put under their pillow. I'm not sure if it's supposed to be a cure for insomnia or a love philter, but she swears they work."

"Does she wear a hat when she mixes the stuff? Don't tell me—it's black and pointed, isn't it?"

"White and pointed, maybe. Actually, when she wears a hat at all, it's orange straw, all covered with flowers and fruit. I think it dates back to her trousseau, circa 1950."

"Hmm," was Fate's rather skeptical comment as they turned down Cadiz Street on a zigzag course that would take them through the oldest part of town on their way to Sophie's favorite breakfast spot.

"Fate," she said diffidently, "Please don't underestimate Flo. She's really a wonderful woman, and besides, she needs me."

Taking her hand, Fate curled his fingers through hers and squeezed gently. "If you say so, honey."

"I like being needed. Living with Flo is almost like having a child to raise. I never know what she's going to be up to next—sometimes it can be pretty hair-raising. I owe her more than I can ever repay, even if sometimes I do wish..."

"You wish?" Fate prompted. He wished, too. Just lately his wishes had been confusing the hell out of him.

Sophie sighed and ducked under a flowering bougainvillea that billowed out over a fence and half the sidewalk. "Well, I can't help wishing that just once I could call home and say, Flo, put the casserole in the oven, or the clothes in the washer, or whatever—and come home later to find that she'd not only put it in—or on, but she'd also *turned* it on!"

Fate threw back his head and laughed, and Sophie, her fingers still entwined in his, leaned her head against his shoulder, unconsciously storing the moment away in her memory.

"A little flaky, huh?" he asked, not unkindly.

"It's my fault. You'd think after all these years of dealing with people, I'd learn to give explicit, step-by-step instructions, leaving nothing open to misinterpretation. Comes of being so bossy all those years when I was in charge of the typing pool. Everyone knows how I like things done, and they're scared stiff of my bark, even though I don't have a bite."

Fate squeezed her hand and said nothing. There were so many holes in her armor by now that he seriously doubted she'd ever be able to lord it over the staff the way she had in the past. Her Serene Highness, indeed! His delightful little Sophie.

"Fate, have you ever heard of something called *huevos rancheros*? I think it's supposed to be Mexican." She rushed on. "It's wonderful! You really ought to try it. You won't want to eat eggs any other way."

Fate considered his answer carefully. There was no way he was going to tell her that Turbyville was possibly the only town with a population of more than five thousand that didn't have at least one restaurant that featured some version of the Mexican breakfast favorite, even if it was little more than catsup on scrambled eggs. "Have you ever traveled much, Sophie?" he countered.

"I've been to Augusta and Columbia, of course. And Myrtle Beach. I almost went to Atlanta once when I was eleven to see this asthma specialist, but by the time they could get an appointment and finish all the paper work for the county health department, I'd already cured myself."

He frowned. They passed the plaza, with its statue, monuments and cannons, and he didn't spare it so much as a glance. "You had asthma? What do you mean, you cured yourself?"

"We turn here; it's in the next block. Just what I said—I cured myself. The vaporizers didn't help much, the medicine made me sick, and I got tired of hearing my cottage mother say it was all in my head. I decided if that was the case, I'd just think myself well. It worked, too—eventually. Of course, there were a few lapses. I wasn't what you might call a model child, and occasionally I got into more trouble than I could handle, and then I wheezed. Growing up is such a messy process, isn't it," she asked as matter-of-factly as if they'd been discussing eating ice-cream cones at the Fourth of July picnic.

Fate stopped short and turned, grabbing her shoulders. "Hold on there, you lost me. Just where the hell did you grow up, anyway?"

"Why—Dunwoody Farm," said Sophie, frowning slightly. "I thought you knew."

Fate felt as if a mule had kicked him in the belly. Dunwoody Farm. The local children's home. How the devil could he have worked with her all this time, and lived in that hotbed of gossip, and still missed that single, telling fact? "Sophie, I'm sorry," he said, his voice rough with feeling. "I didn't know."

Sophie tilted her head and stared at him. "Well, for goodness' sake, don't *you* start. There's nothing wrong with coming from Dunwoody. It's no fancy finishing school, but it's hardly a reform school, either. Once we get enough money together to remodel the kitchen and cafeteria, and maybe hire another full-time counselor—"

"But you were sick!" Fate accused. The sidewalks were filling with tourists, who looked at them curiously and continued on their sight-seeing way. "Who the hell was supposed to be looking after you? Where were the authorities? What was—"

"Oh, for Pete's sake, don't get in a swivet. Come on, if we don't eat something soon, I'll *really* be sick."

With obvious reluctance Fate let himself be moved. "A swivet?" he repeated when Sophie stalled in front of the window of a wax museum.

"One of Flo's terms. Since I've never been in one, I'm not exactly sure what it means. Do you think that's real hair he's putting on that wax head?"

"Sophie, do you want breakfast, or do you want to see the museum?"

"I want breakfast, but I want to see and do everything else, too. Only I don't suppose we have time. Tomorrow we go home, and then it's back to toting barges and lifting bales." She pointed out the café, and he ushered her inside and found them a table.

"Now what was all that about toting barges and lifting bales?" he asked after the waitress had taken their order.

"Just an old song," Sophie dismissed airily. "I don't remember the title, all I know is you get a little drunk and then you land in jail. Fate, I'm so glad you ordered the *huevos rancheros*. I hope you like it."

Some time later, fed and changed, they were headed for Anastasia Island and the beach. Sophie had charmed the chef out of his recipe for the mildly spicy tomato sauce he'd ladled over the fried eggs, and was looking extremely pleased with herself. "You liked it, didn't you?"

"I liked what?" Fate asked. He'd given up trying to do any serious thinking while he was with her. His powers of concentration had been scuttled as neatly as the Spanish had scuttled the French more than four hundred years earlier on this very spot.

"The *huevos rancheros*, of course. Didn't I tell you it was great?"

He muttered something ambiguous, not having the heart to tell her he'd had better Mexican food cooked by a Swedish chef on an aircraft carrier in the North Atlantic. Another symptom. They were adding up at an alarming rate. First the feeling of possessiveness, now this feeling of protectiveness.

They voted unanimously to try the beach at Fort Matanzas State Park rather than return to the beach where Sophie had spent the previous day. "If you'll show me how to ride the waves without a surfboard, I'll go with you to see the fort," Sophie bargained. Her attempts at body surfing the day before had resulted in little more than a complete loss of dignity and a bathing suit full of gravel.

"I doubt if there's much of a surf."

"Try, though, okay? I think I can do it with a few pointers and just a little more practice."

But no amount of practice would make up for a lack of decent waves. A few hours later, Sophie, her shoulders pink and her hair plastered across her face, jutted her chin forward for added momentum. She steadfastly refused to quit without riding just one wave all the way to the shore.

"All right, my indomitable little water-sprite, get the hair out of your eyes so you can see where you're going and get ready to hop aboard this next one."

Sophie leaned forward, bracing for the gentle swell that broke the otherwise smooth surface of the water. Her bottom came in contact with Fate's thighs as he attempted to steady her against the slight current, and she resisted the urge to wiggle it. The truth was that as much as she hated to give up, she was far too distracted to think about riding anything.

Except possibly him. Last night had been so wonderful she could hardly bear to think about it for fear it had all been a dream.

"All right, get ready now," he ordered, his voice sounding oddly strained. "I'll skip this one—it's a little anemic for my weight, but you go ahead."

She actually did go forward, at least a few feet. The trouble was, she also went down. Waterlogged and laughing, she slogged ashore. "I give up," she panted. "I'm just not meant to be a surfer."

"Too much buoyancy," Fate said with a judicious—and faintly licentious—glance at her breasts.

Sophie jerked her straps back into place. "Buoyancy!" she snorted, flopping down on her beach towel. "It didn't feel very much like buoyancy when my face was scraping the bottom. I've even got sand in my eyelashes."

Fate dropped down beside her on the towel he'd bought when they'd stopped for drinks and snack foods, turning so that he was gazing down on her face. "Close your eyes and I'll see if I can clean you up before you blind yourself."

Sophie closed her eyes, knowing full well that he was going to kiss her. It was downright scary, the way she was coming to crave his kisses. She'd reasoned it out quite thoroughly this morning while she'd waited for him to come back to the motel; they'd have this time together, this brief holiday, and then they'd go back home and she'd be Mrs. Pennybaker again and he'd be Mr. Ridgeway, and pretty soon he'd go back to New York and she'd start getting used to another CEO.

Chamus would be the third in as many years—or would it be the fourth?

Sophie had made a firm decision to put the whole thing out of her mind once it was ended. She wouldn't have lost anything, so there'd be no reason to cry or pitch a fit or any of those other emotional outlets a woman might justifiably resort to under extreme stress. You can't lose something you never really had.

"Are you frowning because you know I'm going to kiss you, or because the sand finally blinded you?"

"The sun just went behind a cloud."

"All the more reason to kiss you," Fate said, the corners of his mouth lifting in a teasing smile. He lowered his face until his lips hovered just above hers, his breath fanning her cheeks. Moisture glistened on his tangled lashes, and he smelled of salt water and sun-warmed flesh.

Sophie filled her senses with the sight, the feel, the sound and the scent of him. Her hands slicked down his back until the tips of her fingers just reached the top of his navy briefs. She'd almost collapsed when he'd shucked off his jeans and she'd seen how magnificent he looked in nothing but trunks and an open white shirt.

"The shadows are back," he whispered a hair's breadth from her lips.

"Impossible. The sun's gone behind a cloud. I thought you were going to kiss me."

"I'm holding back in order to build up a demand. I've heard it's a pretty effective sales technique."

"If you build up any more demand, you might not be able to satisfy it," Sophie warned, growling. She hardly recognized the woman she'd become in the past twenty-four hours, teasing, laughing, enjoying her own brazenness.

Fate's tongue slipped between her lips and he slanted his head over hers. One of his legs crossed over hers so that she could feel the fire just waiting to be stoked.

She stoked it. With hands, lips and tongue, with the small movements of her body that told him more clearly than words how much she wanted him, Sophie gave in to temptation and became the temptress.

Aeons later Fate lifted his head. His breathing sounded like canvas being ripped apart, and there was a dazed expression on his face. "Unless we can arrange for a private cell for two in the local lockup, I think we'd better take a quick dip—in the Arctic Ocean, preferably—and then head for the fort."

Feeling every bit as dazed as Fate looked, Sophie tried to rationalize her own behavior. Here they were on a public beach in broad daylight, and she was wallowing in the sand with a near naked man. Sophie Pennybaker, who'd striven all her life to be a model of deportment!

What was even worse, she hadn't even the grace to be embarrassed. When Fate got to his feet, jogged down to the surf and plunged in, all she felt was an overwhelming sense of disappointment.

Nine

Sophie knew that if she were a painter, ten years later she'd have been able to capture every nuance of that magical day. She'd taken one last look at the ocean before they'd gathered up their belongings for the short trek across the highway to the other side of the island, seeing a surf turned milky green against a rapidly graying sky. On the other side of the sliver of land, where live oaks sprawled across neatly kept grounds at the visitor center, she'd insisted on exploring the boardwalked nature trail that led a short distance through swamp and scrubby maritime forest, although most of the foliage was familiar to her. Fate had kissed the mosquito bites on her neck, and they'd lingered, glad for the moment of relative privacy—kissing, touching, and willing time to slow down—until a blast of thunder and a sudden pelting shower had sent them racing for shelter.

Sophie knew she'd never forget the sight of Fort Matanzas against a backdrop of sullen dark clouds, with bolts of lightning stabbing the earth around it. How incredibly small it had looked across the river on its own tiny island. When they'd learned that the last ferry trip across the narrow expanse had been canceled because of the weather, she'd been disappointed, but more for Fate's sake than her own. Actually, the idea of tramping along a swampy path between boat landing and fort on a place called Rattlesnake Island wasn't all that appealing even without the lightning.

The storm blew over quickly, with more fireworks than actual rain. They watched it pass offshore, sitting on a narrow white-sand beach hungrily devouring the oranges, peanuts and cheese crackers they'd bought earlier.

Sophie discovered another facet of Fate's personality as he filled her in on the stormy history that had pitted nation against nation in a battle for religious and territorial expansion. "You'd have made a wonderful teacher," she told him, licking the salt from her fingers.

"I'm afraid teaching calls for more in the way of patience than I can lay claim to. I just happen to be interested, that's all."

They watched a gull dive-bomb the tiny structure. "It's so small. I don't know why, but that makes it seem all the more real to me. History books always made places seem so big and impersonal."

Chuckling, Fate tucked the pop cans, wrappers and orange peels back in the cooler and stretched out with his head in her lap. "To a child's eye, maybe. When's the last time you cracked a history book? When you were twelve? Fourteen?"

"I read history," Sophie said indignantly. "Just last month I was reading a history of patent medicine." She brushed a pine needle from his chest, and then covered the place with her warm palm to protect it from other falling objects.

"Seriously, people really were smaller then. And weapons were a helluva lot bigger. Most of the poor devils probably had hernias before they ever got to the front."

"It's all so sad. Wherever they are, I hope they know people still remember."

They fell silent as thunder rumbled off into the distance, under the eerie spell of a tiny fort that had guarded an inlet for more than four hundred years. Sophie smoothed the dark unruly hair back from Fate's forehead. It was stiff with salt, as was hers. She didn't care. She knew she'd treasure this day as long as she lived. Fate had shared a part of himself with her that she suspected he shared with few other people.

"I wish I'd had time to see a few museums and some of the old Spanish houses," she said wistfully.

Fate rolled over onto his side, kissing her stomach through her damp bathing suit. "We can always come back again."

A tactful response, she thought, smiling down at him, but of course they wouldn't. And she knew she wouldn't come back without him. "Look over there! I do believe the sun's going to shine again," she said with determined cheerfulness. "You know what that means, don't you?"

"I'm afraid to ask," he replied, peering sleepily up at her through a hedge of dark lashes.

"We could have one last dip before we go back to town."

"Woman, you're insatiable." With a groan, Fate got to his feet, then turned and pulled her up, catching her in his arms.

"I'm too sandy to get in the car without rinsing off," Sophie said, laughing. "It's going to take a fire hose to get all the sand unstuck from my carcass as it is."

Fate rubbed a slightly gritty cheek against hers. "I could never abide sandy carcasses in my bed. Remind me to run you through a car wash on the way back to the motel."

"You may as well wax and buff me while you're at it—a lady likes to feel well groomed."

From this day on, Sophie decided, she'd always love the scent of sunscreen and salted peanuts. Sand, sweat and damp bathing suits had never felt so wonderful as they did when Fate held her in his arms. There on the narrow beach, with the trees crowding them toward the water's edge, she poured out her heart in a long, melting kiss, telling him of her feelings in the only way she dared. He didn't have to love her in return. He'd never promised her anything, and she could never ask. Love had to be given freely or it wasn't love.

As if deliberately drawing out time to deny its passage, they swam until both were exhausted. Sophie made up in enthusiasm for what she lacked in skill, and Fate tactfully refrained from commenting on her lamentable style. His own technique was simple and powerful, propelling him through the water with a minimum of fuss and splash.

"If I'd been smart," she panted, raking wet hair back from salt-reddened eyes, "I'd have conned you into giving me a swimming lesson instead of trying to do something more spectacular. I've always been a lousy swimmer."

"What are you talking about, honey? You swim like a regular statue of Poseidon."

"Thanks a lot! At least I don't have to worry about pigeons," she retorted.

The blaze of sunset had turned the swirling suds a creamy shade of coral by the time they waded ashore, laughing and clinging together. Sophie tucked another picture into her mental album.

Fate flung the driest of the towels over her head and rumpled her hair until she grabbed him about the waist to keep from falling, which led inevitably to another long, hungry kiss.

"My God, Sophie, I won't be able to last until we get back to the room at this rate," he groaned, his eyes feverish as he gazed down at lips still dewy from his kisses.

"Oh, is this some sort of an endurance trial?" she teased, all innocence. "You should've told me."

"Come on, let's just get out of here before lust overcomes my better judgment. The park service takes a dim view of people using their property for activities not specifically condoned."

Sophie pulled on her beach wrap and shook the sand from her scuffs. "You mean there's one of those little signs with the red line through it forbidding *that*?"

Laughing, Fate leaned forward and sunk his teeth with exquisite tenderness into the sensitive curve of her neck, and Sophie collapsed against him, trembling with the crazy chain reaction he invariably set off each time he touched her. She'd learned more about her body in the past twenty-four hours than she'd learned in all the previous thirty-three years.

On the drive back up the length of the island, she closed her eyes and tucked her knees up beside her on the seat. She was deliciously tired, floating on a sea of euphoria. Just over the horizon of her consciousness, coloring her thoughts the warm pink of a setting sun, was the anticipation of what still lay ahead. Their last night together. She'd make the most of...

Her eyelids drifted down, fluttered once, and stayed shut.

"Huh? Oh, what—?" Her head jerked up and she blinked.

Fate tossed a tiny paper bag into her lap, grinning as he buckled his seat belt and started the car. They pulled out onto the highway, and Sophie craned her neck to see why they'd stopped at—a pharmacy?

"Brought you a present," he said.

"A present?"

"Something we can both enjoy, actually—but later on, okay?"

He'd bought her a present from a pharmacy? Sophie rubbed the sleep from her eyes. And then it suddenly hit her. She felt the hot rush of blood rise up her neck and over her face. Holding the bag between thumb and forefinger, she dropped it onto the seat between them.

"Thank you," she said stiffly.

"'Course, I wasn't sure what kind you liked. There's a lot more to choose from these days than there was when I was a kid."

A muffled sound escaped her throat. She sat up straight, crossed her ankles, and folded her hands on her lap. For goodness' sake, she scolded herself silently, stop acting like such a ninny! He was just being responsible, she told herself. It was really a very considerate thing to do, certainly nothing to be embarrassed about. Everyone knew what they were. And what they were for. She *couldn't* be the only woman in captivity who'd never had occasion to see one—in person, so to speak.

"I hope you like the flavors I picked out," Fate went on, and Sophie closed her eyes, oblivious for once to the beauty of the colorful Saint Augustine waterfront. He picked up the sack again and tossed it back into her lap. "Go ahead, check it out. I bought some of every brand they had, but if you've got a special favorite I missed, we can always stop in town and—"

"Fa-ate," Sophie wailed.

He had to be teasing her. They both knew she was hardly a woman of the world, but did he have to rub it in? And if he wasn't teasing, why then he was even more blasé than she'd thought.

They parked in their usual slot at the motel, and by the time they'd gathered up their sandy possessions and plodded up the stairway, Sophie was willing to forgive him for his tactlessness. Three days ago, the fact that he had a sense of humor at all would have come as a surprise, although after seeing that video he'd done for the auction, she should've guessed.

"Ever hear the old saying about many hands making light work?" Fate asked. He'd unlocked her door, and while Sophie adjusted her air conditioner, he was giving the beach towels one last shake before bringing them inside.

"Sure. You can make light work by rolling those up and putting them in the laundry bag. They won't dry until I wash the salt out, anyway."

"Okay, and in the interest of getting some dinner before midnight, I'd be glad to offer my assistance in removing the sand from your—uh, carcass."

Compressing her lips, Sophie did her best to look disapproving. It was a sorry best. "Fate, would you please go to your own room and do whatever you're going to do to get ready for dinner? We didn't even have a real lunch, and I'm famished!"

Fate slung a beach towel around her, capturing both ends to draw her close. Green eyes aglow, he said, "I'll let you manage by yourself, sweet Sophie. *This* time. But only because I'm hungry, too, and like I said, if we got in that bathtub together, it would be midnight before we ever got around to going for dinner. By that time, I'd never even make it to the door."

Sophie sagged against him, feeling the blatant need in every line of his body. "That's not what you said, but never mind, I'm in no mood to quibble."

"Maybe not now, but keep in mind, any time you find yourself in a quibbling mood, I'm your man," he murmured suggestively, and shaking her head, Sophie freed herself. At this rate, they'd die of malnutrition.

The minute the door closed behind him she hurried to the bathroom to start the water running. The sooner they got ready, the sooner they'd have dinner, and the sooner they finished that, the sooner...

Tossing her beach wrap at the plastic laundry bag provided by the establishment, she rifled through the few dresses she'd brought along, finding nothing that pleased her. Suddenly all her clothes seemed stodgy and old. The slacks were the youngest-looking things she owned, but she wasn't in the mood for slacks tonight. She wanted to look feminine and desirable.

Finally she decided on the pink jacket-dress, but without the jacket. Perhaps her chunky white beads and the bit of tan she'd accumulated through all that sunscreen would make it look more glamorous. And she'd wear her hair down.

Taking the dress from the hanger, she pawed through her underwear and selected a white lace-trimmed set. At least her underwear wasn't stodgy. Nothing spectacular, but nothing to be ashamed of, either.

She tossed them on the bed, and at the same time, her gaze fell on the small paper sack Fate had left behind. "That wretch!" she cried, laughing in spite of herself. It wasn't the first time she'd been put in charge of an evening's entertainment. She'd often arranged something for the rather informal professional group she belonged to, but usually it had consisted of a reading, or an educational tape, or even a few tables of bridge. This was the first time it had included anything like... *those*!

Sophie found herself reaching for the sack. All right, dammit, so she was curious. People talked about the things in public these days—they even taught school children about them. It was a perfectly commonplace commodity, nothing to be embarrassed about. She'd seen the ads, of course, but she'd always averted her face when she'd passed by that particular display at Harnett's Drugstore, because she could just imagine what Etta Louise Jacocks who worked behind the counter would tell people if she saw Sophie examining the merchandise on the rack just to the left of the pipe tobacco.

"Flavors," she muttered, grabbing the bag and ripping the stapled top open. "He must really think I'm dumb!" Turning it upside down over the bed, she dumped out the contents, half-a-dozen or so small packages, some flat, some round....

"Bubblegum?" she murmured blankly. "*Bubblegum!*" And then she flung herself across the bed and laughed until her sides hurt.

It was after ten when they wandered back to the motel. As the restaurant Fate had picked out was only a few blocks away, they'd walked, deliberately prolonging the period of delicious anticipation.

Sophie identified the various plants, trees, and shrubs they passed, and Fate told her about the cannons, the monuments, and the significance of some of the street names. A horse cart passed, and she gazed after it. "That's something I wish I'd done, too. Mr. Forbus, the farm manager at Dunwoody, used to let me ride the wagon behind the tractor, and I'd always pretend the tractor was a Clydesdale named John, Dear. We weren't supposed to fool around with the farm equipment, except for the older boys, and I always got punished for it, but I did it anyway. It was worth doing without bread pudding for a week."

"We could hire one now. Would you care to take a moonlight tour of the city, Ms. Pennybaker?"

Her hand clasped in Fate's, Sophie sent him a shy look. "Not particularly, Mr. Ridgeway."

He grinned. "Neither would I."

Sophie excused herself to brush her teeth as soon as they got back to her room. When she came out again, Fate was standing beside the bed, grinning down at the lineup of bubblegum across the pillows.

"I wasn't sure what flavor you like best," Sophie told him gravely. "You can have all the grape and orange ones. The original flavor's my very favorite, and I like cherry, but not banana. That tastes like cleaning fluid."

Fate moved up behind her and wrapped his arms about her waist, drawing her back against him so that her head fell naturally into the hollow of his shoulder. "Wanna know what my favorite flavor is?" he whispered, stirring tendrils of hair against her cheek. "Sophie Pennybaker. Right here—" He tasted the spot just under her ear. "And here." His lips followed the curve of her jaw, and she arched her throat. "And—right here." He turned her in his arms and brought his mouth down on hers.

Sophie waited until the very last moment before closing her eyes. Foolish or not, she wanted to savor the look of Fate's green eyes darkening with desire as he bent to kiss her. She knew she'd never forget the lean lines of his muscular body sparkling wet in the sunlight, the way he threw back his head when he laughed, and his sooty eyelashes all spangled with sunlit water when he came up from a dive. Memories were hers to keep.

"Oh, Sophie, sweetheart, you don't know what you do to me," he whispered huskily against her lips.

She knew very well what she was doing to him. Physically, at least. The signals were unmistakable, and her own body responded to those signals as if—

What was it she'd read in FloBelle's old book of knowledge? As if she were a flower about to be fecundated, all swollen and moist and aching to be pollenated, stamen to pistil.

Fate wove his fingers through her hair, muttering something about silk, and waste, and laws against hairpins. He found the buttons at the back of her dress and deftly unfastened them, sliding the soft knit garment off her shoulders.

The evidence of his desire set fire to her senses, but Sophie was no longer shocked at the responses they were able to elicit from one another. It was as if she'd awakened from a dream that had lasted all her adult life, only to find that it hadn't been a dream after all.

"Sophie, Sophie, have I told you today how beautiful you are to me?" Fate traced the lacy border of her bra, hooking his thumbs under the narrow satin straps.

"I think you m-mentioned what a wonderful swimmer I was, but beautiful? Noooo," she crooned as he found her nipples and began stroking them into aching arousal. "I don't believe that came into the conversation."

Somehow they managed to fold back the covers and fall across the bed without releasing each other. Fate had stepped out of his moccasins and removed his shirt, but he still wore the white cotton slacks that set off his dark good looks so well. Packets of bubblegum tumbled around their shoulders, and he brushed them away. "Do you know how hard—how much trouble I've had resisting temptation all day long? With you wearing that little blue bathing suit that showed every line of your body—"

"What did you want me to wear to swim in, a raincoat?"

"Every time you rose up out of the water, your breasts were all budded up, and I wanted to touch them. I wanted to taste them. I wanted..." He lowered his head and began stroking one nugget with his tongue, sending streaks of lightning to her loins.

Sophie had stifled more than a few desires, herself. With Fate wearing a skimpy pair of trunks that fit like a glove—*everywhere*—it was no wonder she hadn't been able to concentrate on water sports. If she'd thought to take along a pair of sunglasses, she'd have probably spent the whole day ogling him and missed the rest of the sights entirely.

By the time all their clothes had been removed and the last packet of bubblegum swept off onto the floor, Sophie was throbbing with a need so great it was almost frightening. Last night had been wonderful, but this was different. What if he—

"Fate," she whispered. "You'll tell me if I do anything wrong, won't you? It's been a long time for me."

Holding her breathlessly tight, he rolled over so that she was lying on top of him. "Darling, there's no way you could possibly do anything wrong. There's no right or wrong about this, you know. As long as we both enjoy it, that's all that matters. I gave you pleasure last night, didn't I? And I think you know just how much I enjoyed it, how much I want you now."

It was embarrassing to talk about it, but she owed him that much. "It's just that—well, I happen to be a very strong woman," she confided. "Some men find that threatening."

Fate grew still. "Your husband?"

She nodded silently and let her head fall onto his shoulder so that she didn't have to look at him. She'd explain, and then, if he decided not to take a chance on her, she could just slide over onto her side, and he could leave, and she'd catch the next barge headed downriver to points unknown.

"You want to talk about it?" His voice was gentle, his hand as he stroked her hair, as light as the touch of a bird's wing.

"Phil was—well, he was what you might call a nonaggressive sort of man. Probably why he wasn't very successful as a salesman," she added with a wavery smile.

"So you were married to a business failure, and your so-called strength threatened his masculine ego. Is that what you're trying to say?"

"It's not so-called—I am strong. I've always been strong, and Phil resented every promotion and raise I got. Finally I stopped even telling him. But about the other... You know what I mean. I don't think Phil was ever all that interested in that sort of thing. Not with me, at least. Oh, he was always kind to me, and we hardly ever argued, but once after we'd sort of made love, he said—well, he said I was too aggressive for a lady, and that it was no wonder he couldn't get in the mood with me climbing all over him and yelling in his ear." The last few words came out in a rush, in a tone so low it was barely audible.

Fate swore softly and with great skill, all the while holding her so tightly she could scarcely get her breath. "And you believed him? You let a pathetic excuse for a man like that color your whole opinion of yourself?"

"Well, I really am sort of bossy, you know. And I— I did make noises. I know I did. It's been years and years, but I can still remember. Fate, it was so *mortifying*!"

Fate turned them so that he was lying beside her, his face no more than a few inches from hers as he gazed into her eyes. "Sophie, most men don't want to sleep with a woman so passive he can't even tell if she's awake. Making love can be anything you want it to be— fast or slow, fierce or gentle." He smiled, his eyes unusually bright. "Noisy or quiet. Just so long as it's not indifferent."

Sophie gave a long, shuddering sigh. "I just thought I ought to tell you. I'm not used to talking about this sort of thing, but with you, it's different."

"I'm glad. I'd hoped it was." He buried his lips in her hair, stroking her back and exploring the twin dimples at the base of her spine. "Honey, haven't you ever talked things over with another woman?"

"Who, FloBelle? She's his mother, for goodness' sake."

"But you've got friends. Surely there's somebody you could—well, women are supposed to discuss things, aren't they? In the interest of mental health and all that good stuff?"

"In *Turbyville*? If you read *Cosmo*, everybody in town thinks you're fast. They're nice people, Fate, don't misunderstand me, but it's just not the sort of place where you air out your personal problems. Everybody knows everybody, and they're all much too interested in everything that goes on."

"Yeah, I noticed that. They all like you though, Sophie."

"They should," she replied, with only a trace of bitterness. "I've provided them with enough entertainment over the years."

"Speaking of entertainment, if we're ever going to get to enjoy our bubblegum, don't you think we should get on with this other business and get it out of the way?"

Swallowing the painful lump in her throat, Sophie stared intently into his eyes. "Oh, Fate, I do—um, believe you're right."

She'd almost told him. Her whole body was aching with the love she felt for this wonderful man who was strong enough to be gentle, and so understanding that she felt more secure in his hands than she ever had in her whole life. The least she could do in return was not burden him with that.

Fate led her tenderly down the pathway to ecstasy, lingering to savor each pleasure along the way. The first time he came into her, Sophie was too tense to find release. There was no way he could hold back, and afterward he held her and apologized.

"Please, darling," she whispered, placing a finger over his lips. "It gave me so much pleasure to know that I could give *you* that much pleasure. I've got lots of patience. Sooner or later, I'm bound to catch on."

"Like you caught on to surfing?"

"Was it my fault the waves weren't big enough to ride?"

"I don't believe I'll touch that one," he teased, and then he kissed her again, slowly, deliberately lighting small brushfires that quickly blazed out of control.

Sophie grew more daring as Fate lured her skillfully past the fences thrown up by years of conditioning. She wanted to explore him as fully as he explored her, to return his caresses full measure, but it took every bit of courage she possessed just to follow his lead. Branching out on her own was simply beyond her.

"Don't you trust me, Sophie?" Fate asked once, sensing her hesitancy even as he encouraged her tentative advances.

"It's not that. It's just—something inside me won't let go." She was leaning back against his thighs, facing him, as he leaned against hers. There was a look of strain on his face as he fought to control the raw passion that raged through his body as her fingers trailed nervously down toward the danger zone.

She tried to explain. "Maybe I'm missing some vital gene or something. Or maybe I had too much Miss Manners and not enough Dr. Ruth when I was growing up. Now, the harder I try, the more impossible it seems."

"Stop trying so hard," Fate suggested, his lips playing over her knee as his fingertips explored the silken inner side of her thigh.

"But I *do* want to—well, to succeed," she said earnestly, and he chuckled. "It's like reaching for a rainbow. When you don't know any better, you're so sure you can touch it, even though the faster you run after it, the farther away it moves. And then you grow up, and you discover what everyone else has always known. It's an illusion. Only a fool would try to catch an illusion."

His voice husky with warmth, Fate whispered, "The trick is not to try." His hands slid up her arms and he shifted her down onto the bed. Following her down, he pressed kisses into the sensitive hollow at the curve of her shoulder as he mounted her. "Close your eyes and relax, love. I'll show you what rainbows feel like from the inside."

Never had Sophie been more aware of a man's superior strength as Fate fought to harness his own fierce desire. His patience and gentleness was his gift to her.

With exquisite care, he transported her to the very threshold. "I almost caught it," she panted as he collapsed across her damp body. "I could feel it all around me, so close—" She broke off, unable to believe she was lying in bed with a man, calmly discussing how close she'd come to arriving at that fabled destination.

Well...calmly was hardly the proper term to describe the sweat-drenched, throbbing condition she found herself in at the moment. Besides, she rather suspected Fate was asleep, but when she tried to ease out from under him, he tightened his grip and rolled over onto his side, carrying her with him. At least she hadn't made any unseemly noises.

Feeling both satisfied and unsatisfied—a situation Sophie put down to having brushed too close to a rainbow—she dozed, her face against Fate's chest, his arm comfortingly heavy on her waist.

Sometime in the night, he awakened her. Evidently, he'd been awake for some time, because by the time Sophie realized she was no longer dreaming, he'd driven her all but mindless with his skilled touch, his tormenting kisses, his exquisite little lovebites.

This time it started as soon as he came into her, as a warm glow of color, pulsating in the distance, and then it grew brighter, so intense she was blinded by the beauty. Gasping for breath, she raced after it, all inhibitions forgotten.

"Oh, please, please!" she cried frantically.

"Slowly, darling—close your eyes and relax, I'll bring you the rainbows," Fate urged, his voice almost unrecognizable as he lifted her higher and higher.

"It's too late!" She couldn't wait, she couldn't go slowly. Her legs tightened around him and her eyes widened with astonishment as wave after wave of shuddering splendor broke over her. Sophie's cry was a soft cascade of sound, Fate's single word, part sigh, part groan.

"Sophie!"

Ten

The change began even before they boarded the plane for home. Having slept late, Fate and Sophie settled for coffee and Danish from a machine and got down to the business of packing and checking out. With a flight to catch, she told herself, there was a perfectly valid reason for not dawdling. She didn't feel much like talking, either.

But by the time they reached Jacksonville and turned in the rental car, it was as if their beautiful day on Anastasia Island and the two nights of breathtaking intimacy had never happened.

Fate seemed preoccupied, if not downright morose, and Sophie tried not to let it hurt. He wasn't moody, and he wasn't being cruel, she rationalized. He was simply more experienced in this sort of thing than she was, but she was learning. Fortunately they were both sensible, mature people. Otherwise, it could easily have become a sticky situation.

She stole a glance at him as he took a file from his briefcase. She happened to know that it was not one that required his immediate attention. Furthermore, he probably *knew* she knew!

Message received, loud and clear, she fumed silently. He didn't have to hammer it home, dammit. While Sophie had never considered herself an overly sensitive person, her ego wasn't made of cast-iron.

"Do you smell French lilacs?" Fate asked suddenly.

"Do I what?" Like a snail, it took her a few moments to emerge from her protective covering. "You don't think this is the same plane, do you?"

"Either that or the baggage compartment is leaking. I sealed the damned things up in three layers of plastic bags, but I'm afraid by now everything in my suitcase is smelling of lilacs."

"Fate, I'm really sorry," Sophie said, impulsively reaching out to touch his hand.

Turning his own hand palm up, he laced his fingers in hers, and for a moment, Sophie thought she saw something in his eyes besides that shuttered look that had grown more pronounced with every mile they put between themselves and Saint Augustine. Before she could explore it further the seat-belt light came on, and then they were busy securing for the landing and the moment passed. She'd probably just imagined it anyway.

Sophie prepared herself for another mild panic attack that never quite happened. Maybe she was becoming a seasoned veteran—at least where flying was concerned.

If she'd needed a final reminder that their whole trip had been little more than a public-relations gesture, she had only to see Petra George and her camera ready to record their arrival.

"God, I'd forgotten the red-eyed barracuda," Fate muttered, gripping her elbow hard enough to cut off the circulation.

"Try to smile," Sophie suggested. "If she gets what she wants, maybe she'll leave us alone." But when he put his arm around her and bared his teeth for the camera, Sophie could have cried. Somehow the public embrace only cheapened what had been so private and so perfect, however brief.

"Hi, kids, welcome home," Pet called out, angling for a shot that would include a part of the cabin and a stewardess. "What, no leis? No sombreros?" *Flash-click, flash-click.* "At least you two managed to get some sun. Mac Bonner slipped on a wet deck and broke his collarbone, and his date was seasick the whole three days."

"Where the hell does she think we were?" Fate grumbled. "Come on, let's get out of here!"

"Sophie, can you work up a smile for our readers, or are you too bummed out after all those dusty old museums?" *Flash-click, flash-click.*

"Don't you have enough pictures yet? We still have a forty-five minute drive, remember," Sophie said the moment her made-to-order smile faded. "I'm sure you're in a big hurry, you probably have several important assignments waiting on you."

"A wedding, a prom, two funerals, and another one of those cozy affairs at the country club where I'm the only unescorted woman there, and I spend half my time trying to piece together a story and the other half trying to look like I'm just waiting for a friend to fight his way through the mob at the bar."

"Maybe you should take a friend next time," Sophie suggested, stepping outside the circle of Fate's arm.

"Hey, are you kidding? You've seen the local talent. Believe me, alone is preferable. Unless... How about it, Ridgeway, wanna carry my camera and keep me from looking like a wallflower?"

"Sorry, but I'll be busy until it's time to head north again. If that's all you need from us, we'll push off," Fate said tersely.

Sophie watched the brief interplay between the two of them, shocked to feel a hot tide of jealousy wash over her. Petra was obviously interested, Fate just as obviously not. But there'd be other Petras, and one day, he *would* be interested, and she didn't want to think about it.

Funny, Sophie thought, hurrying to keep up with the tall man striding through Columbia's airport—it hadn't occurred to her to brace herself against something like this.

Fate retrieved his car from the parking lot and they headed south. Sophie half expected to see Pet George's disreputable orange pickup trailing them, but at least they'd been spared that. She pretended to doze as an excuse not to have to talk, which only made her more susceptible to all the insidious doubts she'd thought she had taken care of so neatly.

Since leaving Florida that morning, she'd come full circle, from wanting to throw herself at him and beg him to try and learn to love her, to being cool, but polite, to being icily dignified. Knowing she wouldn't be able to maintain the pose until he left, she'd settled on handing in her resignation and then being friendly, but reserved, until it took effect.

Dammit, she'd been the one foolish enough to fall in love. It was up to her to fall out of it with as little damage as possible.

Fate insisted on taking her bag upstairs, and Sophie, her composure firmly restored, thanked him politely for the lovely weekend. "I expect I'd better get those wet beach towels in the laundry before they ruin everything in my suitcase. I'll return yours as soon as it's dry, all right?"

"Oh, hell—!" He looked ready to fly off the handle at the slightest excuse, and Sophie clamped her lips shut, determined not to offer him that excuse. "I'm going to stop by the office. I'll see you tomorrow," he said curtly.

"Oh. Okay, I'll just change and come on down then."

"No!" Fate scowled at an inoffensive watercolor she'd bought for practically nothing at a sidewalk art show in Myrtle Beach. "I mean, that won't be necessary, Sophie. Stay here and recuperate. Tomorrow will be soon enough to get back to work—or even the next day."

"But, Mr. Ridgeway—"

It slipped out unconsciously, and Sophie was appalled. So was Fate, if looks were anything to go by. In two quick strides he was beside her, and then he took her in his arms, burying his face in the hair she still wore down around her shoulders, holding her as if he'd never let her go.

But then he let her go.

"I'll see you tomorrow, Sophie, whenever you feel like coming in. I've got a lot of calls to make, and I won't be needing you anytime soon."

Which was about as close as he could come to telling her it was definitely over without actually telling her to get lost, Sophie thought with a bitter little twist of a smile. She listened to the sound of his soft-soled shoes hurrying down the stairs, heard the screen door slam, and then a few moments later, the sound of his car driving off as if the Hound of the Baskervilles were on his tail.

So. That was it, she told herself, striving for a philosophical note to leaven her misery. It seemed that no matter what plans her head made for getting out of this thing with her dignity intact, her heart was determined not to let her off so lightly.

It was just before dark that she found the note. She'd just finished hanging out a line of laundry—washing away the memories of Anastasia Island, she thought, still striving for the philosophical viewpoint. She opened a cabinet to take down a glass for iced tea, and there curled up in one of their five matching iced-tea glasses was a single sheet of paper.

Mildly curious, Sophie switched on the overhead light and propped her elbows on the cool porcelain surface of the sink drain-board while she read it. She hadn't been too surprised when there'd been no one home to welcome her back. Of the two women, Flo had by far the most active social life.

Dearest Sophie,
I was right all along about Mr. Ridgeway, wasn't I? He was the King of Spades right next to the

Queen of Diamonds, surrounded by all those hearts. I feel sure he's a Scorpio, so don't expect him to tell you everything, but with all your Neptune, you'll sense anything worth knowing, anyway. I believe there's some Taurus there, too—he has that Venus dimple, but he definitely doesn't have Libra hips. I wouldn't be surprised if he has a cluster of planets in Capricorn, either, which means he'll age well and be a good provider for you. Now honey, he'll be stubborn, but that's not a bad trait in a good man. My poor sweet Philip was never strong enough for you—too many of the wrong planets in water signs just quenched all that poor boy's fire. With his moon placed the way it was, he was always drawn to strong women, but I'm afraid they only ended up reminding him of his own weaknesses. So you can see why I'm going, Sophie. Now that you have your Mr. Ridgeway and you don't need me to look after you any longer, I'm going to go help Philip and his new family make a go of that restaurant she inherited. I do believe being a father might be just the thing my boy needs, don't you? I'll always love you, Sophie, and you know in your heart if you ever need me again, all you have to do is meditate and I'll feel it. Love always.

Your friend,
FloBelle O'Reilly Pennybaker.

Sophie was stunned, but she managed to read the postscript, which was scribbled across the bottom and along one side, to the effect that the bus driver couldn't take all her boxes of books, so would Sophie please see that they got to New Mexico?

She made herself a pitcher of iced tea and took a glass of it out into the backyard. It was the coolest place around, but it was still sweltering. There wasn't a scrap of a breeze anywhere, and off in the distance, heat lightning flickered incessantly.

FloBelle had left because Sophie no longer needed her? *Who* had been taking care of *whom* all these years? *Who* had stayed behind after Phil had run off, to look after a woman who literally hadn't enough common sense to come in out of the rain, much less to support herself?

With a short laugh of disbelief, Sophie raked her hand over one of her wind chimes, as if eliciting the sound would produce a breeze. Against a dark background of somber pines, her laundry hung limply on the line, like so many small ghosts. She plopped herself down in one of the old metal garden chairs she'd repainted just this spring, enjoying the momentary coldness on the backs of her thighs.

"I'd better remember to fill the bird feeders before I go to work in the morning," she said matter-of-factly. And then she began to swear.

To think that she could have gone anywhere in the world she wanted to go, and started fresh, with nothing of the past to hold her back. Without the constant reminders that her own mother had given her away—that no one else had wanted her enough to try to work through the red tape to adopt her—and that her own husband, pitiful excuse for a man that he was, had preferred a widow six years older than he was, with five children under twelve years old!

She'd thought she was so strong? That wasn't strength that had kept her plugging away all these years, it was sheer stupidity! And as if that weren't enough, she'd almost made the mistake of thinking that Fate might be interested in more than just a brief fling.

Oh, yes, you did, Sophie—admit it! Even knowing she was courting disaster, she'd allowed herself to believe that telling her about his family, talking about all sorts of things that had nothing to do with work—laughing together, playing together, making love together, he might suddenly realize that she meant more to him than he'd thought.

Bare feet resting on dew-wet grass, Sophie clutched her glass until the ice melted and the tea grew tepid. By the time she went inside to shower and go to bed, her plans were made.

"Look, I know it's short notice, but—well, hell, Harry, you're old enough to feed yourself without a nursemaid, aren't you? Didn't you tell me Ola had kids somewhere in Brooklyn Heights? She won't want to relocate, and there's really no reason why she should."

A few minutes later, Fate slammed down the phone, no closer to a solution now than he'd been when he'd called the home office to try and talk Chamus out of bringing along his own secretary. He'd thought it was worth one last shot. The way things stood now, one of the two women would have to be made personal assistant. Harry was going to want to promote Ola Margolis, but Fate knew damn well Sophie would be more valuable to him in the position by virtue of her knowledge and experience at KellyCo. Besides, he wanted it for her. She'd worked hard all her life, she was more than qualified, and now she might get passed over through no fault of her own. And there wasn't much he could do about it, except maybe prepare her in advance.

So far he hadn't even found the courage to tell her about Ola's coming. The truth was, he kept hoping the older woman would back out, or Harry would change his mind. If he wanted her around to look after him, why the devil didn't he marry her? His wife had been dead now for almost fifteen years.

By the time his stomach told him it was long past dinner hour, Fate was no nearer a solution. The only fair thing to do was to let Sophie in on what was going on. She was a sensible woman, perfectly capable of figuring the odds and making her own decisions.

Sophie...

Fate leaned back in his chair, his lips curling in a smile as he thought about the few days just past. Who would have expected things to turn out the way they had? Not that he hadn't taken trips with women before, but there was something about those few days with Sophie that set them apart. He couldn't quite put his finger on it, but he'd felt...comfortable with her. As if they were friends as well as lovers.

Naturally, working with her as closely as he had for the past four months, they'd got to know each other. At least he'd thought they had. But then, he'd suddenly looked at her that first night when they'd got back from having dinner, and it was as if he'd never seen her before—as if a stranger had been hiding inside that cool, serene exterior all these months. The crazy thing was, the more he saw of that stranger, the more he felt as if he'd known her forever.

Abruptly he got to his feet, causing the chair to squeak in protest. The only fair thing to do under the circumstances was to tell her what was going on. Lay the cards on the table and leave the decision to her. He'd insist on a raise in salary for her whether she was promoted or not. He wouldn't mention that part of the deal, of course. Let her think it was Harry's idea.

All thought of food was forgotten as he turned off on River Street and drove the dark length to the last house on the right. There was a light on upstairs, but none in the lower rooms. The white witch must be asleep already, or she was out stuffing her potions and philters under the pillows of unsuspecting victims.

Fate rapped on the door and listened. Then he rapped again. Surely Sophie wouldn't be sleeping at this hour. It was only—he slanted his wrist to the feeble sliver of moonlight that shone through the clouds—a bit after ten.

"Sophie!" he called softly through the screen. "FloBelle?" The screen was hooked, but the front door was standing wide open. He'd have to find some tactful way of letting her know that even in a town like this, it paid to be cautious.

"Fate? Mr. Ridgeway? Is that you?"

"Sophie, let me in, will you? I need to talk to you, and I don't particularly want to broadcast what I have to say to the whole neighborhood."

She came down the stairs like a slender wraith, her hair drifting around her shoulders and something white and loose flowing out behind her. She was barefooted, and she looked anxious. "What's wrong, Mr. Ridgeway?"

"For God's sake, Sophie, stop it! We're not in the office now."

Sophie's lips tightened, but she held on to her temper and her determination not to let this man get under her guard again. "Fine. Have you had anything to eat, Fate? You look hungry." He was still wearing the same clothes he'd worn home earlier that day. Evidently he hadn't even been back to his rooming house since they'd got to town.

"Yeah, matter-of-fact, I could do with something if it's not too much trouble."

"I'll scramble you some eggs then," she offered, making a mental note to substitute low-fat cottage cheese for half the eggs. Fate had told her his father had died of a heart attack, but she hadn't noticed him watching his cholesterol intake. He'd turned into a real barbecue fan in the short time he'd been in Turbyville.

He watched while she moved about the kitchen. "That's pretty," he said after a while. "That thing you're wearing."

Sophie slid the egg-and-cottage-cheese mixture into the pan and glanced down at the white cotton gown with the embroidered birds and flowers. "Thank you. Phil sent it to FloBelle, but it didn't fit, and so she gave it to me."

He toyed with the table knife until she slid the steaming mound off onto a warm plate and popped two slices of whole-wheat bread in the toaster. "Coffee or low fat milk?" she asked.

Fate shrugged. "Milk, I guess. I'll sleep better."

Taking a chair across the table, Sophie waited. He'd been so eager to talk to her that he'd practically rattled the door off its hinges, but now he didn't seem to have anything to say. Or maybe he was just too busy wolfing down his supper, she thought, a knot forming inside her that was part pain, part pleasure. Funny, the feeling of satisfaction a woman could get from watching a man eat a meal she'd prepared. It hadn't been the same with Phil, because he was such a finicky eater.

"Would you like to come upstairs?" she asked after she'd put the dishes in to soak. "We could sit out on the deck. It's cool out there this time of night."

"Don't you have air-conditioning?"

"We have ceiling fans. Once I discovered that pollen didn't bother me, I could never get enough of open windows. Besides, I like to be able to hear my birds and wind chimes."

"Real country girl, aren't you?"

Sophie, who'd been leading the way from the kitchen to the stairs, turned to confront him, her eyes flashing angrily. "Is that a problem, Mr. Ridgeway? If my rural background interferes with my work, I assure you, it won't be a prob—"

"Sophie, I'm sorry. I didn't mean that the way it sounded."

"I don't know why you came all the way out here at this time of night, but I'm sure it's nothing that can't wait until tomorrow. If you've had enough to eat, I won't keep you any longer."

Fate raked a hand through his hair. "Dammit, Sophie, you're deliberately trying to pick a fight, and I won't have it! I came here because—well, because I needed to talk to you about something. Something's come up at the office—I mean, there's this situation with Chamus and a woman he knows. Well, actually, she sort of works for him..."

He tortured his hair again, and Sophie waited, her patience severely eroded. She'd hoped she wouldn't have to see him again outside the office. She had it all planned out, her explanations ready, all arguments covered. With her armor securely in place, she could explain precisely why she'd seen fit to hand in her resignation and apply for the position of assistant administrator at Dunwoody Farms. She'd planned to do both tomorrow.

"So he needs a larger house, is that it?"

"No, dammit, that's not it! I'm trying to explain, but it's not a simple matter."

"All right, Fate, since you're already here, I'll listen to whatever you have to say, but I'm tired and sleepy, so unless it's a real emergency situation, you'd better make it short and sweet."

Looking extremely harried, Fate took a deep breath and squared his shoulders. It was going to be tricky. Evidently, Sophie was not in a mellow mood. "Okay. I've met Chamus a few times, but he came to Bannerman while I was in Seattle, so I don't know a whole lot about him other than the fact that he's a natural for KellyCo because he has a background in textiles and twenty-seven years in management."

"Is this really necessary? I'm aware of Mr. Chamus's credentials." Sophie looked pointedly at the zodiac clock Flo had left behind. Her foot began to tap.

Fate started to speak, stopped, and then began again. "The fact of the matter is, Sophie, I wondered if you could see your way clear to marry me."

The silence was deafening. Sophie almost fell back under the shock of his words, and Fate looked almost as stunned. As if he couldn't believe what he'd just heard.

Sophie recovered first. "Fate, my sense of humor went off duty hours ago. Now if that's all you came for—"

He reached out and grabbed her hand. "No, Sophie, wait! Look, I—" He swallowed hard. Hell, he hadn't meant to say that. That had been the *last* thing on his mind.

Just as taking her to bed had been the last thing on his mind when they'd boarded the plane for Jacksonville, a small voice whispered inside his head. Just as going through with that crazy date idea had been the last thing on his mind when he'd let himself be talked into doing the auction in the first place.

"Fate, I think you'd better go home. It's been an awfully long day, and you didn't get a whole lot of rest while we were gone." As she remembered precisely why he hadn't gotten much rest, Sophie felt a blush begin at the base of her throat and rise to her hairline. With commendable firmness, she added, "We can talk tomorrow, but you may as well know that I've decided to try something new for a change."

"Something *new*! What do you mean, something new?" Fate looked so indignant that Sophie almost smiled.

"I was going to tell you tomorrow, I've accepted the position of assistant director at Dunwoody, beginning as soon as I've worked out my notice."

"The hell you have!" he exploded.

Sophie went on as if he'd never interrupted. Technically, she was getting a bit ahead of herself, but under the circumstances, she felt justified. Besides, she was almost sure she would be hired. The pay was abominable, and there was no one else even interested, as far as she knew. "There are several well qualified executive secretaries at KellyCo, any one of whom can take my place. Besides, I've had to get used to so many different men over the past few years I don't think I can handle another one." At the unintentional double entendre, her lips tightened. "You know what I mean," she mumbled.

"Sophie, you didn't answer my question. Will you marry me?"

She closed her eyes and took a deep breath, praying for the strength and judgement not to give in to overwhelming temptation. He was so darned determined to do the honorable thing, she thought with a surge of tenderness that nearly tore her apart. "No, but thank you very much for asking me," she said very gently.

Fate's shoulders fell. If there'd been a chair near by, he would've collapsed on it, but they were still standing in the hallway beside the stairs, with the smell of incense and all those candles and colored beads cluttering up the windows. "Is it FloBelle? You don't want to go off and leave her? She can come, too. Hell, I'll even adopt her if I have to."

Sophie laid a hand on his arm, shocked to find him tense as coiled steel. "Fate, I appreciate what you're trying to do, but it really isn't necessary. I'm not an innocent young girl, remember? You didn't seduce me, and you don't have to do the honorable thing by marrying me."

He started to speak, but she waved him to silence, knowing that if she didn't have her say and get him out of her house as quickly as possible, she would lose her nerve, and probably a lot more besides.

"Look, I'll be just fine. I've made all sorts of exciting plans for the future, and now, I really have to say good-night. We're going to be swamped with work tomorrow. Everything piles up so when you're gone."

Fate turned away, swore fiercely, and then swung around. The fire in his eyes was unmistakable. "Let's get our facts straight, lady. In the first place, age has nothing to do with anything. As for being innocent, most kids right out of high school know more than you do, and hell no, I didn't seduce you! You've been seducing me with that cool little smile of yours and those tricks you use, like deliberately not wearing revealing clothes and not using perfume, from the first day I walked into that office. I wasn't born yesterday. I can tell when a woman's trying to get my attention. Well, all I'm saying is, it worked," he ended bitterly.

Sophie's mouth dropped open. "That's the most absurd thing I've ever heard in my life. Do you honestly believe what you just said? Are you so egotistical that you think every woman on earth is out to get you?"

"You deny it?"

"Deny it! Of course I deny it!" Sophie threw up her hands in defeat. Who knows, maybe she had been trying all along to attract his attention. According to Flo, such things were preordained, and sometimes the two victims were the very last to know. "Fate," she said, veering erratically from exasperation to amusement, "just tell me one thing. Do you love me?"

"Do I—?" He looked dumbstruck. Round one to the home team, Sophie thought with a miserable sort of satisfaction. "Hell, I don't know what you call it. I've never been in love. But I can tell you this much—if loving means liking someone more than you've ever liked anyone else, trusting them, thinking about them constantly and wanting to be with them every minute of the day and night; if it means lusting to a degree you never even dreamed was possible, then I guess I must be in love. Because that's the way I feel about you. Just a brief summary, you understand—I haven't had time to work up a detailed report."

Fate was thunderstruck at his own words. He'd come here blindly, driven by something he didn't even try to analyze, and he'd thought it was on account of her job. It hadn't been that at all. Trust Sophie to get to the heart of the matter as calmly and efficiently as she did everything else.

Did he love her? Hell yes, he loved her! And now he was scared stiff, because the next move was up to her, and if she didn't feel the same way about him, he didn't know where to go from here.

"Would you like to come upstairs?"

His heart slammed against his rib cage and resumed its erratic pace. "Sure, why not?"

They went directly out onto the deck, and Fate tugged at his loosened collar and leaned against the railing with poorly feigned nonchalance. He wasn't going to say another word. If she was trying to come up with a tactful way of letting him down, he wasn't going to make it any easier for her. He'd give his stock option and a year's salary to know what she was thinking. If he had a clue, he might try psyching her into swinging his way.

No—not Sophie. It would be easier to psych out the Sphinx.

Sophie knew very well what was going on under that thatch of unruly black hair. Hadn't Flo predicted as much? Whether it was due to the placement of her Neptune or a simple case of intuition—if there was such a thing as "simple intuition"—she could almost hear his mind working. She could actually *feel* it, as if she were a seismograph and he was the earth that supported her.

"Fate, you're wondering how I feel about you," she informed him, inordinately pleased to hear herself sounding so calm and serene. She could have sworn that deep down inside, she was turning cartwheels. "You summed up pretty well—I like you, I trust you, I—um, lust for you." For a woman rife with inhibitions, she was doing pretty well, she told herself proudly. Then, acutely aware of Fate's growing tension, she hurried on. "Actually, I do believe it's what they call love, but then, it's so hard to describe intangibles like love and rainbows, isn't it?"

Fate's look of wariness gave way to one of guarded hopefulness, and she crossed the few feet of cool planking and lifted her arms to his shoulders. "Let me put it another way. I'd rather spend just one hour with you than a lifetime with anyone else in the world. And a whole lifetime with you would be all the heaven I'll ever want."

"Ah, Sophie—dear God, how I do love you," he groaned. Holding her fiercely, he began kissing her eyelids, her nose, her cheeks, and her chin. By the time he reached her lips, she was wriggling with pleasure.

"So many things to be worked out," he murmured when they came up for air. "I'll be at the main office when I leave here, and then I'll be moving around—a few months here, a few months there. Could you live in New York until I get ready to move on?"

"If you could handle Turbyville, I'm sure I can manage New York." She eased his shirttail from under his belt and ran her hands over his silky skin until her fingers tangled in the thicket of hair that swirled around his flat nipples. Hearing his sharp gasp when she found what she was seeking, Sophie smiled in the darkness.

Thunder rumbled overhead, and a flash of lightning revealed the ghostlike procession of a line of laundry about to get drenched. "We'll have to spend a few months in Maine," Fate said, leading her inside as the first drops struck.

"That's *way* up north. We'll probably have to cover up, even in the summertime." Sophie switched on the fan over her white wicker bed and drew down the candlewick spread.

"Bannerman's got interests all over the world. We'll travel a lot."

"I've always thought I'd like to travel," Sophie observed thoughtfully as she lifted the hem of her gown and peeled it up over her head. In shedding her inhibitions, she seemed to have shed every bit of modesty she'd ever possessed. Shameful, she thought delightedly. Absolutely shameful!

"Let me help you with that," Fate said huskily, his eyes beginning to glow with a familiar dark gleam. He removed the cotton gown from her arms and then fumbled at his own buttons until Sophie took over the chore.

Moments later, laughing breathlessly, they tumbled onto the lavender-scented cotton sheets. Sophie landed on top and decided the situation had possibilities. "I'm feeling incredibly aggressive. Do you suppose it's because I was already picturing myself as an executive out at Dunwoody?" She heaved an exaggerated sigh that just happened to be aimed at his right ear, loving the instantaneous reaction of his body.

"Keep going," he gritted. "I'll see if I can swing a seat on the board of directors for you."

Sophie slithered down his body until she could reach his nipple with her teeth. "Never mind, love, I think if it's all the same to you, I'll take a break for a few years. I've been working since I was seventeen, and I've missed out on so much. Like a family." She lifted her head. "Could we?"

"You mean—now? It's a noisy process, remember? But if you're sure we won't wake up any sleeping ex-mothers-in-law, I'm game."

"I didn't get around to telling you, but Flo took a bus to New Mexico to live with Phil and his new family." She caught her breath sharply as he shifted until he could reach the place on the back of her knee that drove her out of her mind. "By now—ahhh, Fate, that's incredible! By now," she went on breathlessly, "she's probably naming face cards and casting charts for five new little Pennybakers."

"Does she really believe in all that stuff?" Fate scoffed. By moving only slightly, he was able to pillow his head on the soft hollow between her hip bones. Sophie's heart began to race as she sensed his next move, but she pretended she had all the time in the world for a long, philosophical discussion.

"Hmm. Actually, FloBelle's beliefs are sort of hard to pin down. She believes in everything—or maybe it's just that she doesn't *not* believe in anything."

Fate paused in his lingering journey. "Want to try that again?"

Sophie caught a shuddering breath in her throat as she felt the hot rasp of his tongue in the bend of her thigh. "N-nooo, I don't believe I do."

"What do you want, Sophie love?" he teased.

"Um—technically, we're still on holiday, aren't we?"

"Mmhmm." He kissed her again, with a lingering thoroughness that had her gripping handfuls of goose-down pillow to keep from soaring away into the stratosphere.

"Then could we—could we just concentrate on catching a few more rainbows?"

Fate laughed softly as he gathered her close to his heart. "Rainbows are easy. Tonight, I think we should try for a mirage. Are you with me?"

"Always," Sophie said simply, knowing intuitively that their always would last a lifetime.

* * * * *

Available now

Silhouette Classics

You asked for them, and now they're here, in a delightful collection. The best books from the past—the ones you loved and the ones you missed—specially selected for you from Silhouette Special Edition and Silhouette Intimate Moments novels.

Every month, join us for two exquisite love stories from your favorite authors, guaranteed to enchant romance readers everywhere.

You'll savor every page of these *Classic* novels, all of them written by such bestselling authors as:

**Kristin James • Nora Roberts • Parris Afton Bonds
Brooke Hastings • Linda Howard • Linda Shaw
Diana Palmer • Dixie Browning • Stephanie James**

Silhouette Classics
Don't miss the best this time around!

SCLG-1R

ATTRACTIVE, SPACE SAVING BOOK RACK

Display your most prized novels on this handsome and sturdy book rack. The hand-rubbed walnut finish will blend into your library decor with quiet elegance, providing a practical organizer for your favorite hard-or soft-covered books.

Only $9.95

Approximately 16" x 8" when assembled

Assembles in seconds!

To order, rush your name, address and zip code, along with a check or money order for $10.70* ($9.95 plus 75¢ postage and handling) payable to *Silhouette Books*.

Silhouette Books
Book Rack Offer
901 Fuhrmann Blvd.
P.O. Box 1396
Buffalo, NY 14269-1396

Offer not available in Canada.

*New York and Iowa residents add appropriate sales tax.

Silhouette Romance™
Legendary Lovers Trilogy

BY DEBBIE MACOMBER....

ONCE UPON A TIME, in a land not so far away, there lived a girl, Debbie Macomber, who grew up dreaming of castles, white knights and princes on fiery steeds. Her family was an ordinary one with a mother and father and one wicked brother, who sold copies of her diary to all the boys in her junior high class.

One day, when Debbie was only nineteen, a handsome electrician drove by in a shiny black convertible. Now Debbie knew a prince when she saw one, and before long they lived in a two-bedroom cottage surrounded by a white picket fence.

As often happens when a damsel fair meets her prince charming, children followed, and soon the two-bedroom cottage became a four-bedroom castle. The kingdom flourished and prospered, and between soccer games and car pools, ballet classes and clarinet lessons, Debbie thought about love and enchantment and the magic of romance.

One day Debbie said, "What this country needs is a good fairy tale." She remembered how well her diary had sold and she dreamed again of castles, white knights and princes on fiery steeds. And so the stories of Cinderella, Beauty and the Beast, and Snow White were reborn....

Look for Debbie Macomber's *Legendary Lovers* trilogy from Silhouette Romance: *Cindy and the Prince* (January, 1988); *Some Kind of Wonderful* (March, 1988); *Almost Paradise* (May, 1988). Don't miss them!

Silhouette Intimate Moments

NEXT MONTH
CHECK IN TO
DODD MEMORIAL HOSPITAL!

Not feeling sick, you say? That's all right, because Dodd Memorial isn't your average hospital. At Dodd Memorial you don't need to be a patient—or even a doctor yourself!—to examine the private lives of the doctors and nurses who spend as much time healing broken hearts as they do healing broken bones.

In UNDER SUSPICION (Intimate Moments #229) intern Allison Schuyler and Chief Resident Cruz Gallego strike sparks from the moment they meet, but they end up with a lot more than love on their minds when someone starts stealing drugs—and Allison becomes the main suspect.

In May look for AFTER MIDNIGHT (Intimate Moments #237) and finish the trilogy in July with HEARTBEATS (Intimate Moments #245).

Author Lucy Hamilton is a former medical librarian whose husband is a doctor. Let her check you in to Dodd Memorial—you won't want to check out!